Her frame trem
"It was...terrify
that sound in m

"What's it gonna take for you, Beth?"

"To leave Timberline? The truth. I'm going to leave Timberline when I discover the truth about my identity. Otherwise, what do I have?"

"You have me." He sealed his lips over hers and drew her close.

She melted against him for a moment, her mouth pliant against his. But then she broke away and stepped back.

"I just don't think you understand what this means to me, Duke. It's a lifetime of questions and doubts coming to a head right here. All my questions have led me here."

"You don't know, Beth. It's based on feelings and suppositions and red doors and frogs."

"And that's a start."

He closed his eyes and took a deep breath. He didn't want to take that all away from her—the hope—but he'd snatch it all away in a heartbeat to keep her safe.

SUDDEN SECOND CHANCE

CAROL ERICSON

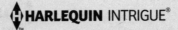

HARLEQUIN INTRIGUE®

For Chuck, one of the most avid readers I know.

Recycling programs
for this product may
not exist in your area.

ISBN-13: 978-0-373-69929-2

Sudden Second Chance

Copyright © 2016 by Carol Ericson

Printed in U.S.A.

www.Harlequin.com

Carol Ericson is a bestselling, award-winning author of more than forty books. She has an eerie fascination for true-crime stories, a love of film noir and a weakness for reality TV, all of which fuel her imagination to create her own tales of murder, mayhem and mystery. To find out more about Carol and her current projects, please visit her website at www.carolericson.com, "where romance flirts with danger."

Books by Carol Ericson

Harlequin Intrigue

Target: Timberline

Single Father Sheriff
Sudden Second Chance

Brothers in Arms: Retribution

Under Fire
The Pregnancy Plot
Navy SEAL Spy
Secret Agent Santa

Brody Law

The Bridge
The District
The Wharf
The Hill

Harlequin Intrigue Noir

Toxic

Visit the Author Profile page at
Harlequin.com for more titles.

CAST OF CHARACTERS

Beth St. Regis—The host of the *Cold Case Chronicles* TV show. She uses the show as a cover to find out if she's one of the missing children of the Timberline Trio, but she runs into a former adversary...and lover, who will either stand in her way or make her forget all about why she's in Timberline.

Duke Harper—This FBI agent is sent to investigate the Timberline Trio cold case, but the dead-end assignment turns into a battle of wits and wills when he meets up with the TV reporter who used him for a story but has been on his mind and in his heart ever since.

Heather Brice—Beth believes she might be this kidnapped child and will stop at nothing to prove it.

Bill Raney—His realty business is suffering due to his chronic drinking and poor business practices, and he's willing to do just about anything to get back on top.

Rebecca Geist—A local Realtor who knows more of Timberline's secrets than she realizes, which puts a target on her back.

Jordan Young—This Timberline mover and shaker is anxious to put the town's dark history in the past, but are his motives civic or personal?

Gary Binder—A recovering drug addict and ex-con, he's either trying to get his life back on track or he's up to his old tricks.

Scarlett Easton—A local artist and native Quileute, she offers to help Beth get in touch with her past, but she pays a price for her generosity.

Serena Hopewell—A bartender at a local restaurant, she owns a prime piece of property in Timberline. Is she a savvy investor or a savvy blackmailer?

Sheriff Musgrove—The new sheriff in town may be a little too cozy with those who would circumvent the law in order to hide the truth.

Chapter One

Beth's heart skipped a beat as she ducked onto the path that led through a canopy of trees. The smell of damp earth and moldering mulch invaded her nostrils. She took a deep breath. The odor evoked the cycle of life—birth, death and rebirth. She'd smelled worse.

She gasped as a lacy, green leaf brushed her face. Then she knocked it away. If she freaked out and had a panic attack every time she delved into the forest, she'd have a hard time doing this story—and getting to the truth of her birth.

Straightening her shoulders, she tugged on her down vest and blew out a breath. She stepped over a fallen log, snapping a twig in two beneath her boot. The mist rising from the forest floor caressed her cheek and she raised her face to the moisture swirling around her.

The scent of pine cleared her sinuses and she dragged in a lungful of the fresh air. She'd definitely classify herself as a city girl, but this rustic, outdoor environment seemed to energize her.

Either that or the adrenaline was pumping so hard and fast through her veins, a massive anxiety attack waited right around the corner.

She continued on the path through the dense foliage, feeling stronger and stronger with each step. She could do this. The reward of possibly finding her true identity motivated her, blocking out the anxiety that the forest usually stirred up inside her.

She'd convinced Scott, the producer of *Cold Case Chronicles*, that she needed to come out ahead of her crew to do some initial interviews and footwork. She had her own video camera and could give Joel, her cameraman, a head start. Stoked by the show's ratings from the previous season, Scott had been ready to grant her anything. Of course, she had a lot of work to do on her own before she got her guys up here. She'd have to stall Scott.

The trees rustled around her and she paused, tilting her head to one side. Maybe she should've researched the presence of wild animals out here. Did bears roam the Pacific Northwest? Wolves? She was pretty sure there were no tigers stalking through the forests of Washington. Were there?

As she took another step, leaves crackled behind her, too close for comfort, and she froze again. The hair on the back of her neck stood up and quivered, all her old fears flooding her senses.

She craned her head over her shoulder and released a gusty breath of air. A man walking a bicycle stuttered to a stop, his eyes widening in his gaunt face.

"Ma'am?"

The relief she'd felt a moment ago that it hadn't been a tiger on her trail evaporated as she took in the man's appearance. He had the hard look of a man who'd been in the joint. She recognized it from previous stories she'd done on her TV show, *Cold Case Chronicles*.

"Oh, hello. My husband and I were just taking a walk. He went ahead."

He nodded once, a jerky, disjointed movement. "Come out to look at the kidnapping site, did ya?"

Heat washed into Beth's cheeks. She wanted to make it clear to this man that she wasn't just some morbid looky-loo, but what did it really matter?

"We were in the area anyway, and it's so pretty out here." She waved a hand toward the path she'd been following. "Is it much farther?"

"Not much." He pushed his bike forward, wheeling around the same fallen log she'd stepped over earlier. "They were lookin' at me for a bit."

"Excuse me?" Beth tucked her hands into the pockets of her vest, her right hand tracing the outline of her pepper spray.

"For the kidnappings." He hunched his scrawny shoulders. "Like I'd snatch a couple of kids."

"Th…that must've been scary." She slipped her index finger onto the spray button in her pocket. "How'd the police get that idea?"

"Because—" he looked to his left and right "—because I'd been in a little trouble before."

Taking one step back, Beth coiled her muscles. She could take him—maybe—especially if she nailed him with the pepper spray first.

"And because I was there the first time."

"What?" She snapped her jaw closed to keep it from hanging open. Did he mean he'd been in Timberline at the time the Timberline Trio was kidnapped? He definitely looked old enough.

"You know." He wiped a hand across his mouth.

"The first time when them three kids were snatched twenty years ago."

Twenty-five years ago, she corrected him in her head.

"You were living here during that time?"

"I wasn't the only one. Lots of people still around from that time." His tone got defensive. "It's just 'cause I had that other trouble. That's why they looked at me— and because of the dead dog, only he wasn't dead."

A chill snaked up Beth's spine. She definitely wanted to talk to this man later if he was telling the truth, but not now and not here in the middle of a dense forest with only the tigers to hear her screams.

"Well, I'd better catch up to my husband. A...are you going to the site, too?"

"No, ma'am. I'm just taking the shortcut to my house." He raised one hand.

Then he turned his bike to the right and her shoulders dropped as she released the trigger on her pepper spray.

"Ma'am?"

She stopped, and without turning around, she said, "Yes?"

"Be careful out there. The Quileute swear this forest is haunted."

"I will and I'm...we're not afraid of ghosts—my husband and I."

He emitted a noise, which sounded a lot like a snort, and then he wheeled his bike down another path, leaving the echo of crackling leaves.

Beth brushed her hair from her face and strode forward. He wouldn't be hard to locate later—an ex-con on a bicycle who'd been questioned about the kidnappings. Maybe he'd have some insight into the Timberline Trio.

She tromped farther into the woods but never lost sight of the trail as it had been well used recently. What was wrong with people who wanted to see where three kids and a woman had been held against their will?

If she didn't have a damned good excuse for being out here, she'd be exploring the town or sitting in front of the fireplace at her hotel enjoying a caramel latte with extra foam, reading—okay, she'd probably be reading a murder mystery or a true-crime book about a serial killer. The Pacific Northwest seemed to have those in spades.

A piece of soggy, yellow tape stirring in the breeze indicated that she'd reached the spot. Law enforcement had drilled orange caution cones into the ground around the mine opening and had boarded over the top. Nobody would be able to use this abandoned mine for any kind of nefarious purpose again.

She nudged one of the cones with the toe of her boot—it didn't budge. Wedging her hands on her hips, she surveyed the area. No recognition pinged in her chest. Her breathing remained calm, too, so nothing here was sending her into overdrive.

Not that she'd really expected it. Wyatt Carson had chosen this place to stash his victims because he'd discovered it or had searched for someplace to hide the children, not because he'd known it from twenty-five years before when he was just a child himself, when his own brother Stevie Carson had been snatched.

But one kidnap story might lead to another. Maybe the Timberline Trio had been held here before…before what? If she really were one of the Timberline Trio, those children obviously weren't dead. So, why had they been kidnapped? Why had *she* been kidnapped?

There was something about this place—Timberline—that struck a chord within her. As soon as she'd seen that stuffed frog in the window of the tourist shop during a TV news story about the Wyatt Carson kidnappings, she'd known she had to come here. She could be Heather Brice, and she had to find out.

Crouching down, she scooted closer to the entrance of the mine. When Carson had found it, the mine had a cover that he'd then blocked with a boulder. All that had been removed and cleared out.

She flattened herself onto her belly and army-crawled between the cones. Someone had already pried back and snapped off a piece of wood covering the entrance.

With her arms at her sides, she placed her forehead against one slat of wood and peered into the darkness below. She'd like to get down there just to have a look around. Maybe the local sheriff's department would allow it if she promised to get their mugs on TV.

A swishing noise coming up behind her had her digging the toes of her boots into the mushy earth. She'd just put herself into an extremely vulnerable position—an idiotic thing to do with that ex-con roaming the woods. A branch snapped. She slipped her hand inside her pocket and gripped the pepper spray, her finger in position.

A man's voice yelled out. "Hey!"

Then a strong vise clamped around her ankle. This was it. In one fluid motion, she dragged the pepper spray from her pocket, rolled to her back, aimed and fired.

The man released her ankle immediately and staggered back, one arm flung over his face.

Beth jumped to her feet, holding the spray in front of her with a shaky hand, ready to shoot again.

Her attacker cursed and spit.

Beth's eyebrows shot up. The ex-con had gotten bigger…and meaner.

Then he lowered his hands from his face and glared at her through dark eyes streaming with tears. Those eyes widened and he cursed again.

He cleared his throat and coughed. "Beth St. Regis. I should've known it was you."

Beth dropped her pepper spray and clasped her hand over her heart. She'd rather be facing a tiger right now than Duke Harper—the man she'd loved and betrayed.

Chapter Two

Duke's eyes stung and his nose burned, lighting his lungs on fire with every breath he took. Even through his tears, he couldn't mistake the woman standing in front of him, her shoulder-length, strawberry blond hair disheveled and her camera-ready features distorted by surprise and... fear.

She should be afraid—very afraid after the way she'd used him.

He kicked at the pepper spray nestled in the green carpet between them. "Is that the stuff I gave you?"

"I...I think so."

"Then I'll count myself lucky because that's expired. You should've replaced it last year, but if you had, I wouldn't be standing upright forming words." He pulled up the hem of his T-shirt to his face and wiped his tears and his nose.

Miss Perfect would hate that he'd just used his shirt as a handkerchief—and that was fine with him. He peered at her through blurry eyes and she still looked perfect—damn it.

She wrinkled her nose. "I'm sorry. I thought you were an ex-con attacking me."

She must be referring to Gary Binder, unless there were other ex-cons in Timberline who lived out this way. He'd already done his homework on the case but he had no intention of sharing his info with her. Oh, God, she had to be here for the same case he'd been assigned to investigate.

He narrowed his already-narrowed eyes. "You're doing a story for your stupid show on the Timberline Trio, aren't you?"

"That *stupid show*, as you call it, got a point-six rating last year, more than half of those viewers in the prime demographic." She tossed her hair over one shoulder as only Beth St. Regis could.

"Junk TV."

She clapped a hand over her mouth, her eyes wide. "Oh, my God. That's why you're here. You're investigating the Timberline Trio."

"What else would I be doing here?" He lifted one eyebrow and crossed his arms. "Do you think I followed you to Timberline?"

Red flags blazed in her cheeks. "Of course not. Why would I think that? What we had was…"

"Over."

"Yeah, over." She waved her hand in the general direction of his face. "Are you okay? I really did think you were that ex-con coming after me. Why did you grab my leg?"

"I thought you were falling in."

"Through that small space?"

"I couldn't see how big it was."

"I was fine. As soon as I heard you coming, I got

ready for the attack. You told me once I needed to be more careful, more aware of my surroundings."

"Good to see you're taking my advice…about something." He ran a hand across his face once more and sniffled. "Where's the rest of your crew, or are you a one-woman show now? I guess Beth St. Regis doesn't need other people—unless she's using them."

Her nostrils flared but she ignored the barb. "I'm doing some prep work. My cameraman and producer will be coming out later."

"And the circus will ensue."

"If the FBI is involved, there really must be something to investigate."

She brushed off her jeans that fit her a little too closely, so he kept his blurry eyes pinned to her face.

"Isn't that why this case is on your radar? You must've heard about the new information we got during the investigation of the copycat kidnappings." He cocked his head. "Come to think of it, I have a hard time believing the old Timberline Trio case is sexy enough for *Cold Case Chronicles*. Maybe *you* followed *me* out here."

Her sky blue eyes widened for a split second and then she giggled nervously, her hand hovering near her mouth. "I have no idea what happened to you after…that last case, Duke Harper. You dumped me, and it's not like I've been following your career or anything like a stalker."

A thrill of pleasure winged through his body at her lie. So she'd been tracking him. What did that say about him that the thought gave him satisfaction? It also meant she knew about the royal screwup that had resulted in the death of his partner, Tony.

"That's okay. I haven't watched one of your shows,

either." The slight lift at the corner of her luscious lips told him she'd picked up on his lie, too.

"I suppose you're not interested in joining forces, are you? Pooling our resources? We're an unbeatable team. We proved that before."

He snorted. She didn't deserve an answer to that one. They'd been an unbeatable team in bed, too, but that hadn't stopped her from playing him.

"What were you doing crawling around on the ground?" He pointed to the cover over the mine.

"Prep work." She sealed her lips. "Where are you staying while you're here?"

"Timberline Hotel."

She raised her hand. "Me, too."

He pasted on his best poker face. "Makes no difference to me."

"Do you have a partner with you or are you working alone?"

A partner? The FBI would have a hard time trying to find someone to partner up with him after Tony. He shoved his hands in his pockets and kicked at a gnarled root coming up from the earth.

"Oh, come on, Duke. Whether or not you're working with a partner is not giving up any classified info."

He shrugged. He had no intention of giving this woman one morsel of information. She should know that working a cold case was like being exiled to Siberia—for him, anyway. This was punishment and he didn't want to discuss his failure with her.

"I guess you'll follow your leads and I'll follow mine." He circled his finger in the air. "How long have you been here?"

"Just a couple of days. I'm trying to get a feel for the place. I even brought my own video cam."

A flock of birds shrieked and rose from a canopy of trees and the hair on the back of Duke's neck stood up. Hunching forward, he crept toward the tree line.

"What are you doing?" Beth's voice sounded like a shout and he put his finger to his lips.

Voices carried in the outdoors and those birds had taken off because something—or someone—had disturbed them. The abandoned mine was in a clearing, but dense forest and heavy underbrush hemmed it in on all sides.

The trail from the road had wound past an abandoned construction site to the clearing, and it continued on the other side. The birds had come from the other side.

He reached the beginning of the trail and took a few steps onto the path, his head cocked to one side. Leaves rustled and twigs snapped, but that could be animals going about their business. His gaze tracked through the blur of green, but he didn't spot any movement or different colors.

City life had his senses on high alert, but a rural setting could pose just as much danger—of a different kind.

He exhaled slowly and returned to the clearing, where Beth waited for him, hands on her hips.

"What was all that about?"

He pointed to the sky. "Those birds took off like something startled them."

"I told you I saw a rough-looking guy out here on a bike. Maybe it was him."

"Doesn't explain why he was hanging around. I don't

know that you should be traipsing around the forest by yourself." He snorted. "You're hardly an outdoor girl."

She kicked a foot out. "I have the boots."

He opened his mouth for a smart-ass reply but someone or something crashed through the bushes and they both jumped this time. Duke reached for the weapon tucked in the shoulder holster beneath his jacket and tensed his muscles.

He dropped his shoulders when three teenage boys came staggering into the clearing, laughing and pushing each other. The roughhousing came to an abrupt halt when they spotted Duke and Beth.

The tallest of the three boys stepped forward, holding a can of beer behind his back. "Is this, uh, official business or something?"

The other two edged back to the tree line, trying to hide their own beers.

"Nope. I was just leaving." Duke leveled his finger at the boy. "But you'd better not be operating a motor vehicle."

"Driving? No way, sir."

Beth flashed her megawatt smile at the trio of teens. "Do you boys live here? I'm from the TV show *Cold Case Chronicles*, and we're doing a show on the old Timberline Trio case."

"Oh, hey, yeah. My mom watches that show all the time."

One of the other boys, a pimple-faced kid with a shock of black hair, mimicked the tagline of the show in a deep voice. "*Cold Case Chronicles*…justice for all time."

"That's us." Beth nodded. "So, how about it? Any

of you know anything about that case? Parents around at the time?"

The one who'd spoken up first said, "Nah, we just moved here a few years ago when my mom got a job with Evergreen Software."

The kid with the acne answered. "Same here."

The dark-haired boy with the mocha skin who'd been quiet up to now ran a hand through his short hair. "My family was here, but they don't talk about it. *We* don't talk about it."

"We?"

Duke rolled his eyes as Beth tilted her head, that one word implying a million questions if the boy wanted to pick one up. The teen had better run now if he wanted to avoid that steam train.

The tall, skinny boy answered for his friend. "Levon is Quileute. They believe in voodoo magic and boogey-men."

Levon punched his friend in the arm and the tall kid dropped his beer where it fizzed out in the dirt. "Hey, man."

All three boys picked up where they'd left off, crashing back into the woods, cursing at each other and laughing, startling a flock of birds with their raucousness.

"Well, that's interesting." Beth tapped the toe of her boot. "I wonder what that boy meant about the Quileute not talking about the crime. Did law enforcement ever question anyone from the tribe?"

"Not that I know of, but I'll leave that to your superior investigative talents." He jerked his thumb over his shoulder. "It's been real, but I gotta go."

"I guess I'll see you around, Duke. We are in the same hotel, same small town, same case."

"Don't remind me." He waved over his shoulder and hit the trail back to his rented SUV, putting as much space as possible between him and Beth St. Regis, his mind as jumbled as the carpet of mulch he was plowing through.

She looked the same, except for the clothes. Beth had always been a girlie-girl—high heels, dresses, manicured nails, perfect hair and makeup. The jeans, boots and down vest suited her. Hell, a burlap sack would suit Beth. She had the kind of delicate beauty that shifted his libido into overdrive.

He'd fantasized about those girls when he was a teen growing up on the wrong side of the tracks in Philly—the rich girls with the expensive clothes and cars, the kind of girl that wouldn't give him the time of day unless she wanted to tick off her parents by running with a bad boy.

He'd been drawn to Beth like a magnet for all the wrong reasons. You couldn't use a living, breathing person to fix whatever you'd missed in your childhood. But, man, it had felt good trying.

When he'd had Beth in bed, he couldn't get enough of her soft porcelain skin, the way her breast fit neatly into the palm of his hand and the feel of her fine, silky hair running down his body.

The thought of those nights with Beth's slim legs wrapped around his hips got him hard all over again, and he broke into a jog to work off the steam.

When he got to the car, he collapsed in the driver's seat and downed half a bottle of water. Just his luck to run into the woman of his dreams on this nightmare assignment.

He dug his cell phone from the pocket of his jacket and called his boss, Mickey Tedesco.

"I was just thinking about you, man. All settled in up there? I hear it's some beautiful country."

"Don't try to sell this, Mick. I checked into my hotel and took a walk in the woods to have a look at where the kidnap victims were held a few months ago, not that those kidnappings had anything to do with the Timberline kidnappings, except that the brother of one of the original victims turned out to be the kidnapper." He dragged in a breath. "Why am I doing this? Doesn't the FBI have more urgent cases that need my attention?"

"You know why, Duke." Mick coughed. "It's always a good idea to ease back into work after a…um, situation."

"I'm good to go, Mickey." His hand tensed on the steering wheel. "I don't need to be poking around a twenty-five-year-old kidnapping case based on some slim new evidence, which isn't even evidence."

"I don't know. It may not have started out too promising, but you might be getting more than you bargained for, Duke. You might have yourself a hot one."

A vision of Beth aiming her pepper spray—pepper spray he'd given her—at his face flashed across his mind. "I might be getting more than I bargained for, all right. That bogus *Cold Case Chronicles* show is out here nosing around."

Mick sucked in a breath. "Beth St. Regis is there, in Timberline?"

"Yeah." Mick knew a little about the drama that had gone on between him and Beth…but not all of it.

Mick whistled. "That makes total sense now."

"It does?" Duke clenched his jaw. "Are they promoing the segment already? She doesn't even have her crew out here."

"No. It makes sense that Beth's doing a show about the Timberline Trio because someone sent us an email about her yesterday."

Duke's pulse skipped a beat. "About Beth? What'd it say?"

"The email, untraceable of course, said 'Stop Beth St. Regis.'"

Chapter Three

Beth parked her rental car in the public parking lot on the main drag of Timberline and flicked the keys in the ignition. Why did Duke Harper have to be here mucking up her investigation?

She chewed her bottom lip. He'd been sent out on a cold case because of what had happened in Chicago. She'd read all about the botched kidnapping negotiation that had ended in the death of Duke's partner, a fellow FBI agent. But Duke had rescued the child.

Tears pricked the backs of her eyes. Duke had a thing about rescuing children…but he couldn't save them all.

She plucked the keys from the ignition and shoved open the car door. She couldn't get hung up on Duke again. This story had presented her with the opportunity to get to the bottom of her identity, and she didn't plan on letting tall, dark and handsome get in her way.

She locked the car with the key fob and dropped it in her purse. The chill in the autumn air had her hunching into her jacket as she walked toward the lit windows lining the main street.

If she recalled from the TV news story on the kidnappings, the tourist shop was located between an ice-cream place and a real-estate office. She started at the end of the block and passed a few restaurants just getting ready for the dinner crowd, a quiet bar and a coffee place emitting a heavenly aroma of the dark brew she'd sworn off to avoid the caffeine jitters. The Pacific Northwest was probably not the best place to swear off coffee.

A neon ice-cream cone blinking in a window across the street caught her attention. She waited for a car to pass and then headed toward the light as if it were a beacon.

The tourist shop, Timberline Treasures, with the same frog in the window, nestled beside the ice-cream place, and Beth yanked open the door, sending the little warning bell into a frenzy.

A couple studying a rack of Native American dream catchers glanced at her as she entered the store.

"Hello." A clerk popped up from behind the counter. "Looking for something in particular?"

"I am." Beth gripped the strap of her purse, slung across her body, as she scanned the shelves and displays inside the store. "I'm interested in that frog in the window."

"The Pacific Chorus frog." The woman smiled and nodded. "Timberline's mascot."

Beth's gaze tripped across a small display of the frogs in one corner. "There they are."

The clerk came out from behind the counter and smoothed one hand across a stuffed frog, his little miner's hat tilted at a jaunty angle. "They're quite popular and these are originals."

Beth joined her at the display and reached for a frog, her fingers trembling. "Originals?"

"These are handmade by a local resident." She tapped a bucket filled with more stuffed frogs. "These are mass-produced but we still carry the local version."

"Is there a noticeable difference between them?" Beth held the handmade frog to her cheek, the plush fur soft against her skin.

The clerk picked up a frog from the barrel. "The easiest way to tell is the tag on the mass-produced version. It's from a toy company, made in China."

"The color is slightly different, too." Beth turned over the frog in her hand and ran a thumb across his green belly. She hooked a finger in the cloth tag attached to his leg and said the words before she even read the label. "Libby Love."

"That's the other way to tell." The clerk lifted her glasses attached to the chain around her neck. "Every handmade frog has that tag on it."

"What does it mean?" Beth fingered the white tag with the lettering in gold thread. "Libby Love?"

"It's the name of the artist, or at least her mother—Elizabeth Love. Libby's daughter, Vanessa, makes the frogs now."

Beth took a steadying breath. She'd already figured her childhood frog had come from Timberline, but now she had the proof. "When did her mother start making the frogs?"

"Libby started making those frogs over forty years ago when Timberline still had mining." The woman dropped her glasses when the browsing couple approached the counter. "Are you ready?"

While the clerk rang up the tourists' purchases, Beth studied both frogs. Now what? Even if she'd had a frog from Timberline, it hadn't necessarily come from this store. And if it had come from this store, any records from twenty-five years ago would be long gone.

The clerk returned with her head tilted to one side. "Can I help you with anything else? Answer any more questions?"

"So, these frogs—" Beth dangled one in front of her by his leg "—this is the only place to buy them?"

"The Libby Love frogs are available only in Timberline, although Vanessa sells them online now."

"How long has she been selling them online?" Beth held her breath. Surely, not twenty-five years ago.

The woman tapped her chin. "Maybe ten years now?"

"Is this the only store in Timberline that sells the Libby Love frogs?"

"Oh, no. All the tourist shops have them and even a few of the restaurants." The woman narrowed her eyes. "They all sell for the same price."

"Oh, I'll buy one from you." Beth studied the woman's pleasant face with its soft lines and had an urge to confess everything. "I...I had a toy like this frog when I was a child."

"Oh? Did your parents visit Timberline or get it from someone else?"

"I'm not sure." Her adoptive parents could've passed through Timberline and picked up the frog, but their taste in travel didn't include road trips through rural America.

"It's always nice to reconnect with your childhood. Can I ring that up for you now or would you like to continue looking around?" She glanced at her watch. "I do close in a half hour."

Sensing a sale, the clerk didn't want her to walk out of there without that frog tucked under her arm. She didn't have to worry. Beth had no intention of walking out of there without the frog.

"I'll look around for a bit." Who knew what else she'd discover in there? With her heart pounding, she wandered around the store. She felt close to something, on the verge of discovery.

Maybe in a week or two she'd be ready to track down the Brices and present herself to them as their long-lost daughter who had been kidnapped from Timberline twenty-five years ago. It would be a helluva story for the show, too.

She couldn't forget about the show—she never did. Being the host of that show had given her the recognition and attention she'd missed from her parents. How could she have put that into words for Duke two years ago without sounding pathetic?

Stopping in front of a carousel of key chains, she hooked her finger through one and plopped it down on the glass countertop. "I'll take this, too."

As the woman rang up the frog and the key chain, she peered at her through lowered lashes. "Are you here to do a story on the Timberline Trio?"

Beth dropped her credit card. "What?"

The woman retrieved the credit card and ran her finger along the raised lettering. "You are Beth St. Regis of the *Cold Case Chronicles*, aren't you? I recognized you right away. My sister and I love your show."

"Th…thank you." Wasn't that what Beth had always

wanted? People recognizing her on the street, praising the show, praising her? Wasn't that why she'd betrayed Duke Harper?

"I...we..."

"Well, I figured it had to be the Timberline Trio case. We don't have any other cold cases around here. Our former sheriff, Cooper Sloane, made sure of that with the kidnappings we just had. Could've knocked me over with a feather when it turned out Wyatt Carson had kidnapped those kids. Why would he do that when his own brother was one of the Timberline Trio?"

"That was...interesting."

The woman put a finger to her lips. "I can keep a secret if you want, but I think most people are going to realize that's why you're here. Timberline is still a small town, despite Evergreen Software. Word will spread."

"It's no secret. I'll be interviewing Timberline residents and visiting all the original locations." Beth signed the credit-card slip. "I'm just doing some preliminary legwork right now and my crew will be joining me later."

Of course, the good people of Timberline would know the purpose of her visit. Word may have already spread, thanks to those boys in the woods. Soon everyone in town would know.

But nobody needed to know her ulterior motive for the story—including Duke Harper.

It would've been something she'd have shared with him two years ago, but now they had too many secrets between them. She'd noticed he hadn't offered up any explanations of why a hotshot FBI agent was wasting his time on a cold case, although she already knew the reason.

Beth hugged the bag to her chest. "Thanks...?"

"Linda. Linda Gundersen."

"You seemed knowledgeable about the stuffed frog. Were you living here when the three children were kidnapped?"

"No. My sister and I took over this shop when we both retired from teaching in Seattle. She'd dated a man from this area for a while, liked it, and suggested it as a place for us to retire." Crossing her arms, she hunched on the counter. "That was fourteen years ago when property was cheap. Turns out it was a good move because things started booming when Evergreen set up shop here."

Beth dug a card out of her purse and slid it across the glass toward Linda. "If you know anyone who'd like to talk to me about the case, have them give me a call."

"I will. My sister, Louise, would love to be on the show."

"Does she know anything about the case?"

"No, but she hired Wyatt Carson to do some plumbing on our house." Linda's voice had risen on a note of hope.

"I'll see if my investigation on the story takes me in that direction. Thanks again."

"Enjoy your frog."

Beth turned at the door and waved, stepping into the crisp night air. Darkness had descended while she'd been in the tourist shop, and her rumbling stomach reminded her that she'd skipped lunch.

Her hotel didn't have a restaurant on the premises

and the yellow light spilling out of Sutter's across the street beckoned.

She had no problem eating alone—her job necessitated it half the time she was on the road, and her nonexistent social life dictated it when she was at home.

The plastic bag in her hands crinkled and she decided to make a detour to her car. If she had a bigger purse she'd stuff her frog in there, but her cross-strap bag had no room for her new furry friend and she didn't want to haul the frog into the restaurant. That part of this story she wanted to keep under wraps until she had more proof.

How many adults looking for answers had made the pilgrimage to Timberline, believing they were Stevie, Kayla or Heather? But she had a strong feeling she'd been here before.

She withdrew the frog from the bag and kissed him before stuffing him back in the bag and dropping it on the passenger seat. She'd kissed plenty of frogs in her day, but this one really was going to make all her dreams come true.

She locked up the car and strode back to the restaurant. It had just opened for dinner and a sea of empty tables greeted her—no excuse for the hostess to stick the single diner by the kitchen or the restrooms. She nabbed a prime spot next to the window, ordered a glass of wine and started checking the email on her phone.

Every time Beth looked up from her phone, more and more people filled the room, and she began to notice a few furtive glances coming her way. Linda had been right. News in a small town traveled fast.

If the locals showed an interest in the story, it would make for some good TV. She and her crew never went into these situations with the goal of actually solving the mystery, although a few times they'd gotten lucky. She'd gotten lucky when Duke had shown up during her story two years ago—lucky in more ways than one.

That *Cold Case Chronicles'* investigation had led to the arrest of a child killer who'd been living his life in plain sight of the grieving families. It had been one of her finest hours...and had cost her a budding relationship with Duke.

When the waitress brought her a steaming bowl of soup, Beth looked up just in time to see Duke walk into the restaurant.

She ducked her head behind the waitress and peered around her arm.

The waitress raised her eyebrows. "Everything okay?"

"Just thought I saw someone I knew."

"In Timberline, that's not hard to do even if you are from Hollywood."

"LA."

"You are that host from *Cold Case Chronicles*, aren't you?" The waitress had wedged a hand on her hip as if challenging Beth to disagree with her.

"I am, but I don't live in..." She shrugged. "Yeah, I'm from Hollywood."

"I wasn't here during the first set of kidnappings but—" the waitress looked both ways and cupped a hand around her mouth "—I could tell you a thing or two about Wyatt Carson. I used to date him."

"Really?" Everyone seemed to want to talk about Wyatt, but that case was one for the books. "Did he ever talk much about his brother and what might've happened to him?"

The waitress's eyes gleamed. "A little. I could tell you about it…on camera. I'm Chloe Rayman, by the way."

"We'll talk before we commit anything to video, Chloe." Beth held out her card between two fingers. "If it's something we can use, I'll have my cameraman film you when he gets here."

"Oh, I think it's something you can use." Chloe plucked the card from Beth's fingers and tucked it into the pocket of her apron.

Even if Chloe didn't have anything of importance to add to the story, the waitress would want her fifteen minutes of fame anyway. Beth's challenge on these stories had always been to separate the wannabes from the people with hard facts. Sometimes the two types meshed.

Beth lifted a spoonful of the seafood bisque and blew on the hot liquid.

"Digging in already, huh?"

She'd taken a sip of the soup and choked on it as she looked into the chocolate-brown eyes of Duke Harper. She dabbed a napkin against her mouth. "Dive right in. It's the only way to do it."

"It's the only way you know."

"I'd invite you to sit down—" she waved at the place across from her "—but I'm sure you have important FBI business."

The wooden chair scraped the floor as he pulled it out. "The only important business I have right now is dinner."

She gulped the next spoonful of soup and it burned her throat. What possible reason could Duke have for joining her for dinner? Maybe he wanted to grill *her* for information this time.

"The seafood bisque is good." She drew a circle around her bowl of soup with her spoon.

Chloe returned to the table, practically bursting at the seams. "Are you Beth's cameraman?"

"Would it get me a beer faster if I were?" Duke lifted one eyebrow at Chloe, who turned three different shades of red.

"Of course not. I mean, what kind of beer would you like?"

"Do you sell that local microbrew on tap here?"

"Yes."

"I'll have that and the pork chops with the mashed potatoes, and you might as well bring me some of that soup she's slurping up."

Beth dropped her spoon in the bowl. "Why did you join me if you're going to sit here and insult me?"

"That wasn't an insult. Are you getting overly sensitive out there in LA? You used to be a tough broad, Beth."

Rolling her shoulders, she exhaled out of her nose. Duke liked to needle her. It hadn't bothered her before—when they'd been in love. But now that he hated her? She couldn't take the slightest criticism from him.

"Pile it on, Duke. I can take it." She set her jaw.

"Relax, Beth. Your slurping made the soup sound good. That's all I meant."

Relax? Was that a jab at her anxiety? She squeezed her eyes closed for a second. If she didn't stop looking for innuendos in his conversation, this was gonna be a long dinner.

She scooped up a spoonful and held it out to him with a surprisingly steady hand. "Try it."

He opened his mouth and closed his lips around the spoon. "Mmm."

Heat engulfed her body and a pulse throbbed in her throat. My God, she couldn't be within five feet of the man without feeling that magnetic pull. And he knew it.

She slipped the spoon from his mouth and lined it up on one side of the bowl just as Chloe brought Duke's beer and another bisque.

"Are you done, Beth?"

"Yeah, thanks." She pushed her bowl toward the eager waitress.

When she disappeared into the kitchen, Duke took a swig of beer and asked, "What's up with the waitress? Is she your new best friend or what?"

"She dated Wyatt Carson and thinks that's going to get her camera time."

"You have that effect on people, don't you? They tend to fall all over themselves in your presence."

She stuck out her tongue at him and took a gulp of wine. She needed it to get through this meal.

"Interesting case, Wyatt Carson." Duke flicked his bottle with his finger.

"I know, right?" Beth hunched forward. "Why do you think he did it? Hard to imagine he'd want to put other families through that hell when he'd suffered the loss of his brother."

"One of two things." Duke held up two fingers. "Either he missed the attention and limelight of those days when his brother went missing or he really did just want to play the hero. He kidnapped those kids and then res-

cued them. Maybe he thought he could get past his survivor's guilt by saving other children when he couldn't
save his brother."

"Twisted logic." Beth tapped her head.

"Do you want a slurp, er, sip?" He held his spoon poised
over his soup. "I had one of yours."

"No, thanks. I have some fish coming."

"Yeah, yeah. I know the camera adds ten pounds.
You still run?"

"There are some great running trails here. Did you
bring your running shoes?"

"Of course. Running is the only thing that kept me
sane…keeps me sane with the pressures of the job."

"Same here." So the loss of his partner must've weighed
heavily on him. Did he suffer from that same survivor's
guilt as Wyatt Carson?

"You doing okay with all that—" he circled his finger in the air "—panic stuff?"

"I'm managing." Did he care? He'd acted like he wanted
to strangle her today in the woods. Of course, she'd just
nailed him with some expired pepper spray.

"How are your eyes? They still look a little red."

"I'm managing."

Chloe brought their entrées at the same time and hovered for several seconds. "Can I get you anything else?"

"Not for me."

Beth shook her head. "No, thanks."

As Duke sliced off a piece of pork chop and swept it
through his potatoes, he glanced around the room. "Does
the entire town of Timberline know why you're here?"

"I don't know about the entire town, but everyone in

this restaurant has a pretty good idea by now, thanks to Chloe."

"Do you think that's a good idea?" His lips twisted into a frown.

"How else am I going to investigate, to get information?" She squeezed some lemon on her fish and licked the tart juice from her fingers.

Duke shifted his gaze from her fingers to her face and cleared his throat. "I guess that's how you operate. Stir up a bunch of trouble and heartache and move on."

Beth pursed her lips. "None of the original families is even here anymore. Wyatt Carson was the last of Stevie's family in Timberline. Kendall Rush, Kayla's sister, blew through town, got caught up in Wyatt's craziness and then hightailed it out of here. And Heather's family... They moved away from Timberline, to Connecticut, I think."

"You've done your homework."

"I always do, Duke."

"What I can't figure out—" he poked at his potatoes "—is why you were attracted to this cold case. It hardly has all the elements you usually look for."

"And what elements would those be?"

"You know—sex, drugs, grieving families, celebrity."

She chewed her fish slowly. Duke hated what she did for a living—had hated it then, hated it now. She didn't have to answer to Special Agent Duke Harper or anyone else.

She drained her wineglass. "I was following the copycat kidnapping story and got interested in the old story, like a lot of people. There seemed to be heightened interest in the Timberline Trio and talk of some new evidence, so I figure I'd capitalize on that. Right up my alley."

"Excuse me, Ms. St. Regis?"

Beth turned and met the faded blue eyes of a grand-motherly woman, linking arms with another woman of about the same age.

"Yes?"

"I'm Gail Fitzsimmons and this is my friend Nancy Heck. We wanted to let you know that we were both living here at the time of the Timberline Trio kidnappings and we'd be happy to talk to you."

"Thank you." Beth reached into her purse for her cards, ignoring Duke's sneer—or what looked pretty close to a sneer. "Here's my card. I'll be doing some preliminary interviews before my crew gets here."

Nancy snatched the card from Beth's fingers. "You mean we aren't going to be on TV?"

Duke coughed and Beth kicked him under the table. "I can't tell yet. We'll see how the interviews go."

When the two ladies shuffled away, their silver heads together, Duke chuckled. "This is going to be a circus."

"And what exactly are you doing to work this cold case?"

"I have all the original case files. I'm starting there." He held up his hands. "Don't even ask. You can do your interviews with Wyatt Carson's ex-girlfriend's ex–dog sitter's second cousin."

"Don't dismiss what I do. I helped the FBI solve the Masters case."

"You helped yourself, Beth."

Chloe approached their table. "Dessert?"

"Not for me." Beth tossed her napkin on the table.

Pulling his wallet out of his pocket, Duke said, "Just the check."

"You paying?" Beth reached for her purse. "I have an expense account."

"And you're using it to pay for your own dinner. I'm using my per diem to pay for mine. I don't want any commingling here."

She lowered her lashes and slid her credit card from her wallet. Was he talking about just their finances?

"Got it." She tapped her card on the table. "No commingling."

A loud voice came from the bar area of the restaurant, and chatter in the dining room hushed to a low level—enough for the bar patron's words to reach them.

"That TV show better not start nosing around. If anyone talks to that host, I'll give 'em the business end of my fist." The man at the bar turned to face the room, knocking over his bar stool in the process.

His buddy next to him put a hand on his shoulder, but the belligerent drunk shook him off.

"Where's she? I'll toss 'er out right now on her fanny. Tarring and feathering. That's what we should do. Who's with me?" He raised his fist in the air.

A few people snickered but most went back to their dinners. Duke didn't do either. He marched across the room toward the bar.

Beth groaned as she scribbled her signature on the credit-card receipt and took off after him. Duke had always been a hothead, and it looked like he hadn't changed.

"What did you say?" He widened his stance in front of the man. "Are you threatening the lady?"

"You with that show, too?" The man looked Duke up and down and hiccuped.

His friend picked up the stool and shoved his friend into it. "C'mon, Bill. Take it easy. Who knows? Being featured on TV might increase our property values."

The man, his dark hair flecked with gray, shook his head and stuck out his hand. "Sorry about that. My friend's a Realtor and has had a little too much to drink. I'm Jordan Young."

"Duke Harper." Duke gestured toward Beth. "This is Beth St. Regis, the host of *Cold Case Chronicles* and the woman your friend was threatening."

Jordan Young dismissed his drunken friend with a wave of his hand. "It's the booze talking. His sales numbers haven't been great lately, but it has nothing to do with the recent publicity we've been getting. Hell, Kendall Rush's aunt's place sold for top dollar. He's just ticked off that he didn't get that listing."

He took Beth's hand in his and gave it a gentle squeeze. "I'm a big fan of the show, Ms. St. Regis."

"Thanks." She nudged Duke in the back. "Are you a Realtor, too?"

"Me?" He chuckled. "Not really. I'm a developer, and I have a lot more to lose than Bill here if things go south, but that's not going to happen—Evergreen Software will make sure of that."

"You need to tell your friend to keep his mouth shut about Beth."

"Duke." She put her hand on his arm. His stint in Siberia hadn't done anything to temper his combativeness. "I'm sure he's not serious—at least about the tar-and-feathering part."

Young winked. "Good to see you have a sense of

humor about it, Ms. St. Regis, but I can understand your...coworker wanting to be protective."

Duke didn't correct him. If the residents of Timberline knew all about *Cold Case Chronicles* looking into the Timberline Trio, they didn't seem to be as knowledgeable about the FBI putting the case back on its radar. Maybe Duke wanted to keep it that way.

"You can call me Beth." Her eyes flicked over his gray-streaked hair and the lines on his face. "Were you here at the time of the initial kidnappings?"

"I was. Sad time for us." He withdrew a silver card case from his suit jacket and flipped it open. "If you're implying you want to interview me, I might be available, although I don't know how much I could contribute."

She took the card and ran her thumb across the gold-embossed letters. "You'd be the first one in town without some special insight."

"Can you blame them?" He spread his hands. "A chance to be on TV and talk to the beautiful host?"

"Thank you." The guy was smooth but almost avuncular. Duke could wipe the scowl from his face, but she didn't mind that another man's attentions to her irritated him.

"You should take care of your buddy here." Duke jerked his thumb at Bill, still resting his head on the bar.

"I'll get him home safely to his wife. Good night, now." Young turned back to the bar. "Serena, can you get Bill a strong cup of coffee? Make it black, sweetheart."

Duke put his hand on her back as he propelled her out of the restaurant—with almost every pair of eyes following them.

As Duke swung the door open for her, Chloe rushed

up and patted her apron. "I'll be calling you, Beth. I don't care what Bill Raney says."

"Looking forward to it, Chloe."

When they stepped outside, Duke tilted his head. "Really? You're looking forward to talking to Chloe about Wyatt Carson?"

"You never know what might pop up in a conversation. Maybe Wyatt remembered something about his brother's kidnapping that he never told the cops."

"Why wouldn't he have told the cops?"

Beth zipped up her vest. "Because he turned out to be a nut job."

"Seems to be no scarcity of those in this town." He hunched into his suede coat, rubbing his hands together. "Where are you parked?"

"In the public lot down the block. This is Timberline. You don't have to walk me to my car."

"Just so happens I'm parked there, too." He nudged her with his elbow. "There have been two high-profile kidnapping cases in Timberline. I wouldn't take your safety for granted here. There might be more people here who feel like Bill."

"I'm hardly in danger of getting tarred and feathered... or kidnapped." She stuffed her hands into her pockets and lifted her shoulders to her ears. She may have already been kidnapped from Timberline once. What were the odds of it happening again?

Duke followed her through the parking lot to her car anyway, occasionally bumping her shoulder but never taking her hand. What did she expect? That they would pick up where they'd left off two years ago? Before he'd accused her of using him? Before she'd used him?

As she reached the rental, her boots crunched against the asphalt and she jerked her head up. "Damn. Somebody broke the window of my car."

"Safe Timberline, huh? Maybe Bill did his dirty work before he hit the restaurant." Duke hunched forward to look at the damage to the window on the driver's side. "You didn't have a laptop sitting on the passenger seat, did you?"

"No, but…" Her ears started ringing and she grabbed the handle of the car door and yanked it open.

Someone had taken the bag from the gift shop. Collapsing in the driver's seat, she slammed her hands against the steering wheel. "My frog. They took my frog."

Chapter Four

Duke's eyebrows shot up at the sob in Beth's voice. Someone had smashed the window of her rental car and she was worried about a frog?

"Beth?" He placed his hand against the nape of her neck and curled his fingers around the soft skin beneath her down vest. "What frog, Beth?"

She sniffled and dragged the back of her hand across her nose. "Some frog I bought in a gift store. I... It's particular to Timberline."

"I'm sure they have more." He released her and braced his hand against the roof of the car. Why was she overreacting about a frog? She must be driving herself hard again, maybe even succumbing to those panic attacks that had plagued her for years.

Because she didn't even know about the warning the FBI had received about her. He'd debated telling her but didn't want to worry her needlessly about an anonymous email. Who knew? The emailer may have sent the same message to Beth or her production company. Maybe that was why she was breaking down over a frog.

"You can replace the frog. Will your insurance fix the window on the rental car?"

"I'm sure I'm covered for that." She leaned into the passenger seat and peeked beneath the seat.

"It's gone?"

"Yep."

He kicked a piece of glass with the toe of his boot. "You're not sitting on glass, are you? The window broke inward, so there's gotta be some on the seat."

"There wasn't." She climbed out of the car and gripped the edge of the door as if to keep herself steady and upright. "He must've brushed it off."

"We're reporting this." Duke pulled his phone from his pocket, scrolled through his contacts and placed a call to the Timberline Sheriff's Department. "We have some vandalism, a broken car window, in the public lot on the corner of Main and River."

He gave them his name and a description of Beth's rental car before ending the call.

"Are they coming?" She cupped the keys to the car in one hand and bounced them in her palm.

"Of course. This isn't LA." He grabbed her hand and held it up, inspecting the dot of blood on the tip of her ring finger. "There *was* some glass in the car. Are you sure you're okay?"

Her wide eyes focused on the blood and she swayed—another overreaction. She seemed to be taking this break-in hard. Maybe she *did* know about the warning against her—and he didn't mean Bill's drunken threats.

Grasping her wrist lightly, he said, "Come with me to my car down the aisle. I have some tissues in there and some water."

By the time they reached his rental, she'd regained a measure of composure. "Idiots. Why would someone go through all the trouble of breaking a window on a rental car to get to a bag of stuff from a tourist shop?"

"Maybe if you hadn't left your bag on the passenger seat in plain view." He unlocked his car and reached into the backseat for a box of tissues, and then grabbed the half-filled bottle of water from his cup holder. "How many times have I told you not to leave things in your car?"

"Let's see." She held out her middle finger. "Must've been a hundred times at least."

"Very funny. It's your ring finger." At least she'd come out of her daze.

"Oops." She held out the correct finger and wiggled it.

He moistened a tissue with some water and held it against the bead of blood. "Apply some pressure to that. Did you get cut anywhere else?"

"Not that I can tell." She tipped her chin toward the cop car rolling into the parking lot. "The deputies are here."

As two deputies got out of the car, Duke whispered in Beth's ear. "That's what I like about Timberline. Two cops come out to investigate a broken window and a missing frog."

She stiffened beside him but a laugh gurgled in her throat.

She'd sure grown attached to that frog in a short span of time...unless there was something else in the bag she didn't want to tell him about. With Beth St. Regis, the possibilities were limitless.

The first deputy approached them, adjusting his equipment belt. "You call in the broken window?"

"And a theft. I had a bag in the car from Timberline Treasures."

The second deputy pointed at Beth. "You're Beth St. Regis from that show."

"Do you watch it?"

"No, just heard you were in town to dig up the old Timberline Trio case."

"I think Wyatt Carson already did that." She jerked her thumb at Duke. "You do know the FBI is looking into the case again, too."

The officer nodded at Duke and stuck out his hand. "Deputy Stevens. I heard the FBI was sending in a cold-case agent. The sheriff already turned over our files, right?"

"Special Agent Duke Harper." He shook hands with the other man. "And I have the files."

The other officer stepped forward, offering his hand as well. "Deputy Unger. We'll do whatever we can to help you. My mother was good friends with Mrs. Brice at the time of the kidnapping. I was about five years older than Heather when she went missing. That family was never the same after that. Had to leave the area."

Beth was practically buzzing beside him. "Deputy Unger, could I interview you for the show?"

"Ma'am, no disrespect intended, but I'm here to help the FBI. I'm not interested in being a part of sensation-alizing the crime. We've had enough of that lately."

"But…"

Duke poked her in the back. "You wanna have a look at the car now?"

"Sure. We'll take a report for the rental-car company

and insurance purposes. Probably a kid or one of our local junkies."

Duke asked, "Do you have a drug problem in Timberline?"

"Crystal meth, just like a lot of rural areas." Unger flipped open his notebook and scribbled across the page.

When they finished taking the report, they shook hands with Duke again. "Anything we can do, Agent Harper."

"Well, they weren't very friendly." Beth curled one fist against her hip.

"I thought they were very friendly."

"Yeah, you get the cops and I get Carson's ex-girlfriend's dog walker's cousin."

"Second cousin's ex–dog sitter."

"Right." She tossed her purse onto the passenger seat of the car and hung on the door. "Thanks for seeing me through the report…and the words of advice."

He was close enough to her that the musky smell of her perfume wafted over him. "Do you want some more advice, Beth?"

She blinked. "If you're dishing it out."

"Find another case for your show. Get off this Timberline Trio gig. Since I'm in the Siberia of cold-case hell anyway, I can even toss a couple of good ones your way."

Her eyes narrowed. "Why would you do that? You must really want me off this case."

"It's not me." Raking a hand through his hair, he blew out a breath. "Someone else wants you off this case."

"What? Who? Bill?"

"We got an anonymous email and I don't think it was from Bill Raney."

"That's crazy. The FBI got an email about little, old me? How did anyone even know I was doing a show on the Timberline Trio?"

"How long have you been in Timberline?"

"Two days."

"We got the email two days ago."

She sucked in her bottom lip. "You think it's someone here?"

"It has to be, unless the station has been doing promo for it."

"Not yet. We wouldn't release anything about a story we haven't even done yet. It might never come off."

"Then it has to be someone here in Timberline or someone related to someone in Timberline. You haven't exactly been shy about your purpose here."

"No point in that. But why contact the FBI?" She snapped her fingers. "It must be someone who knows the FBI is looking into the case, too. Maybe this anonymous emailer figures the FBI will have some pull with me."

Duke snorted. "Mr. Anonymous obviously doesn't know you."

"You know what's strange?"

"Huh?"

"Why didn't this person warn off the FBI? If it's someone who doesn't want me looking into the Timberline Trio, why would this same person be okay with the FBI dredging up the case?"

"I have no idea. Maybe he thinks *Cold Case Chronicles* has a better shot at solving the case than the FBI." He scanned her thoughtful face. "That was a joke."

"It's strange, Duke. I suppose you tried to trace the email."

"With no luck."

"Must be someone who's computer savvy, which isn't hard to find in this town with Evergreen Software in the picture."

He captured a lock of her silky hair and twisted it around his finger. "How about it, Beth? Why don't you back off? I'll find you another case, a better case for your show."

"You don't really think I'm in danger from an anonymous email, do you? I get a lot of anonymous emails, Duke. Some are unrepeatable."

"What about this?" He smacked his palm on the roof of the car. "Someone sends a threat and then someone breaks into your car. Do you think it's a coincidence?"

"Could just be a tweaker like Unger said. Besides, this could be good for you."

"How so?"

"If someone who was involved in the disappearance of the Timberline Trio twenty-five years ago wants me off the case and is willing to harass me about it, you might be able to pick him up and actually solve the case."

"You think I'd use you, put you at risk to solve a twenty-five-year-old case?" He clenched his jaw.

She swallowed, her Adam's apple bobbing in her slender throat. "I…"

"Just because you did it, don't expect the same treatment from me." He backed away from her car. "Drive carefully."

WITH TEARS FLOODING her eyes, which had nothing to do with the cold air coming through the broken window, Beth glanced at Duke's blurry headlights in her rearview mirror.

He hadn't forgiven her, despite his concern for her safety tonight.

Maybe that concern was all a big act. Maybe the anonymous email was a lie. Why would someone want to warn her away from the case but not warn the FBI?

Unless this someone knew her true identity. Did someone suspect her real purpose for highlighting the Timberline case?

She pulled into the parking lot of the Timberline Hotel with Duke right behind her. They even got out of their cars at the same time. He followed her inside, but made no attempt to talk to her.

She dreaded the awkward elevator ride, but he peeled off and headed for the stairwell. Once she stepped into the elevator, she sagged against the wall.

Was the warning to the FBI connected to the break-in? Had the thief grabbed the bag because she'd left it out, or had he wanted to send a message by taking the Libby Love frog? And what was that message?

She slid her card key in the door and leaned into it to shove it open.

She dropped her purse on the single chair in the room and sauntered to the window, arms crossed. Resting her head against the cool glass, she took in the parking lot beneath her.

Did Duke have a better view? If he'd taken the stairs, his room was probably located on the lower floors. The hotel had just five. Who was she kidding? Duke could run up five flights of stairs without breaking a sweat or gasping for breath. The man was a stud, but not the overly muscled kind. He had the long, lean body of a runner.

She banged her head against the window. No point in letting her thoughts stray in that direction. He'd been concerned about her tonight, but that could just be because he wanted her out of the picture.

Little did he know, she had more at stake here than good ratings.

She could tell him, confess everything…well, almost everything. He already knew that she'd been adopted and hadn't been able to locate her birth parents. If she explained to him her suspicions about being Heather Brice, maybe he could help her. Maybe he'd share the case files with her.

She pivoted away from the window. If she told him that now, he'd suspect her of spinning a tale to get her hands on the information he had. She wouldn't go down that road with him again.

Sighing, she swept the remote control from the credenza and aimed it at the TV, turning it on.

With the local TV news blaring in the background, she got ready for bed. Snug in a new pair of flannel pajamas she'd bought for the trip, she perched on the edge of the bed to watch the news. She hadn't made the local news—not yet.

She switched the channel to a sitcom rerun and flipped back the covers on her bed. Her heart slammed against her chest and she jerked back as she stared at the head of the Libby Love frog positioned on the white sheet, his miner's hat at a jaunty angle.

Chapter Five

Beth slammed the frog head on the reception counter, squishing the hat. "Where did it come from?"

The hotel clerk's eyes popped from their sockets. "Ma'am, I'm sorry. I have no idea how it got in your bed. Perhaps it had been washed with the sheets and the maid thought it belonged to you."

"This—" she shook the head at him until some white stuffing fell onto the countertop "—does not look like it's been through an industrial washing machine. It looks brand-new, except for the fact that it's been ripped from its body."

"Ma'am, I don't know. I can talk to the maids in the morning."

"What's going on?"

Beth gulped and swiveled her head to the side. What was Duke doing down here? Might as well get it over with.

"I found this—" she thrust the frog head toward him "—in my bed when I got back to my room."

He held out his hand and she dropped the head into his palm.

"What the hell? Is this the frog you bought earlier that was stolen from your car?"

"Stolen?" The clerk turned another shade of red. "I can assure you, we don't know anything about any theft."

Beth released a long breath. "I don't know if it's the exact same toy I bought, but it's the same kind. So if the thief who broke into my car didn't put it in my room, it's a helluva coincidence that someone else did."

The hotel clerk reached for the phone. "Should we call the sheriff's department?"

Duke tilted his head back and looked at the ceiling of the lobby. "Do you have security cameras?"

"Just in the parking lot, sir. We can check that footage to see if anyone drove into the lot without coming through the lobby."

"That's a good idea. It would've been within the past ninety minutes. Do you have a security guard on duty…" He glanced at the man's name tag. "…Gregory?"

"This is Timberline. No security guard." Gregory lifted his hands. "Sheriff's department?"

"Will they come out for a stuffed frog head?" Beth crossed her arms over her flannel pj's, recognizing the ridiculousness of that statement. At least she didn't feel as if she were choking as she had from the moment she'd seen that frog in her bed. Duke had that effect on her—a calming, steadying presence.

Too bad she had the opposite effect on him.

He gave her a crooked smile. "You heard Gregory. This is Timberline. They'll come out for a stuffed frog. It's not just the head. It's the fact that someone broke into your room and put it in your bed…and the smashed car window before that. You want to report and document all this."

Gregory picked up the phone. "I'll call it in. We may learn more tomorrow when the housekeeping staff comes in. I'll make sure we question all of them thoroughly. The night crew was here until about an hour ago, so they could've been here when the, uh, frog was put in your room."

"Thanks, Gregory." Beth tucked her messy hair behind her ears and flashed him one of her TV smiles. "I'm sorry I got in your face earlier. That frog rattled me."

"I understand, ma'am. If you and the…gentleman—" he nodded toward Duke "—want to help yourselves to something from the self-serve concession while you wait for the sheriffs, it's on the house."

"Don't mind if we do. Thanks, Gregory." She crooked her finger at Duke and then charged across the lobby to the small lit fridge and rows of snacks, her rubber flip-flops smacking the tile floor.

She yanked open the fridge door with Duke hovering over her shoulder. "You're still in your pajamas."

Leaning forward, she studied the labels on the little bottles of wine with the screw tops. "Excuse me. I didn't have time for full hair, makeup and wardrobe once I realized someone had been sneaking around my hotel room beheading frogs."

She wrapped her fingers around a chilled bottle of chardonnay and turned on him, almost landing in his arms. She thrust the bottle between them. "What were you doing wandering around the hotel?"

His dark eyes widened. "Are you accusing me of planting the frog? I was with you, remember?"

"Now who's being sensitive? The thought never crossed my mind, but you were headed toward the stairwell the last time I saw you."

"I stepped outside for some air. My room was stuffy and I couldn't sleep." He held up the frog head. "It's a good thing I did. You looked ready to gouge out poor Gregory's eyes."

"I was spooked." She ducked back into the fridge. "Do you want a beer or one of these fine wines?"

"I'll take a beer." He ran his hand down the length of her arm. "Must've freaked you out seeing that frog in your bed."

She handed him a cold beer. "It did. The fact that it was just his head made it worse. Was that some kind of warning?"

"Is this story worth it?" He took the mini wine bottle from her and twisted off the lid. "For whatever reason, someone doesn't want you digging into this case, and this person is willing to put you through hell to get that point across."

"Would you quit if someone started warning you?"

He twisted off his own cap and took a swallow of beer. "It's different. If someone started warning the FBI off a cold case, it would give us reason to believe we were on the right track."

"Maybe I'm on the right track."

"You just got here. It seems to me that some person or persons don't want a story on Timberline. Having the FBI investigate is a different ball game. Maybe these warnings to you are designed to stop you from dragging the town of Timberline through the mud again. You know, reducing the real-estate prices, like Bill said."

She took a sip of wine. "You saw the people at the restaurant. Most were eager to help."

"There could be two factions in town—one group wants the attention and the other doesn't. The ones that don't want the limelight have started a campaign against you—a personal one." He clinked his bottle with hers. "Give it up, Beth. Move on to something else. I told you. I have the cold-case world at my fingertips now and can turn you on to a new, sexy case."

She took another pull straight from her wine bottle and gritted her teeth as she swallowed. "I'm not going to quit, Duke. I want to investigate this case."

"Evening, Ms. St. Regis." Deputy Unger swept his hat from his head. "Gregory told us you had some more trouble tonight."

"It's the stuffed frog stolen from her car." Duke held out the frog head. "Someone planted it in her hotel room."

Unger whistled. "Someone really wants you gone— I mean off this story."

"Can you check the tape from the security camera in the parking lot?" Beth put her wine bottle behind her back just in case Unger thought she was a hysterical drunk. "Gregory said the hotel had cameras out there. Maybe someone will appear on tape who's out of place."

"I spoke to him on the way in. Gregory's getting that ready for us right now. Let's go up to your room and check it out. See if there are any signs of a break-in."

Duke proffered the frog head on the palm of his

hand. "The frog's been manhandled by a bunch of people, but maybe you can get some prints from it."

Unger pulled a plastic bag from the duffel over his shoulder and shook it out. "Drop it in. We'll have a look."

They all trooped up to her hotel room and Beth inserted the card with shaky fingers. She didn't know what to expect on the other side of the door.

Nothing.

Everything was the way she'd left it, covers pulled back on the bed and the TV blasting. She grabbed the remote and lowered the volume. "It was there, on the middle of the bed, beneath the covers."

Unger looked up from studying the door. "No signs of forced entry. You're on the fourth floor. Does the window open?"

"No."

He had a fingerprinting kit with him and dusted the door handle and the doorjamb. Once he finished asking a few more questions, he packed up his stuff. "I'll have a look at the footage now. If I find anything, I'll let you know."

Duke stopped him. "One more thing, Deputy Unger. A Realtor by the name of Bill Raney was making some threats against Beth in Sutter's tonight."

"We'll talk to him. That man's been on a downward slide lately. I can't imagine him out breaking car windows and sneaking into hotel rooms, but you never know what people will do when their backs are against the wall."

Beth sighed. Why did this have to be happening on the most important case of her life? Maybe if she just explained herself publicly. She honestly didn't care who had kidnapped her twenty-five years ago and she wasn't interested in putting Timberline in the spotlight again. She just wanted to confirm her identity. She wanted to go to the Brices with proof. She wanted to go back to a loving home.

She'd already made a mistake. She should've done her sleuthing on the sly. She should've come to Timberline as a tourist, taken up fishing or hiking or boating. She'd just figured she had the best cover. Nobody would have to know her ulterior motive. Nothing would have to get back to the Brices until she was sure.

"Ms. St. Regis?"

She looked up into Deputy Unger's face, creased with concern. "Are you okay? Gregory offered to move you to another room."

"I think that's a great idea." Duke tossed her suitcase onto the bed. "In fact, the room next to mine on the second floor is empty."

Beth's mouth gaped open. Duke must really be worried if he wanted her rooming right next to him. Today in the forest he'd acted like he'd wanted to strangle her.

"That might not be a bad idea—if you're insisting on continuing with this story." Unger slung his bag over his shoulder and walked to the door.

"Deputy Unger, who exactly doesn't want the old case dredged up from the cold-case files?" Holding her breath, she watched his face. *He* didn't. He'd made that clear before.

He shrugged. "People like Bill. People with a lot to lose—think property values, reputations, businesses—those are the people who want to put this all behind us.

The executives at Evergreen about had a fit when Wyatt Carson kidnapped those kids and struck fear into the hearts of their employees—the people they'd lured here with a promise of safety and clean living."

"I don't see how a crime that occurred twenty-five years ago can still tarnish the luster of a city." She grabbed her vest from the back of the chair and dropped it next to her bag on the bed.

"C'mon, Beth." Duke scratched his stubble. "You've been doing the show long enough to realize what can happen to a town when all the dirty laundry is hung out for everyone to see."

"Maybe I won't end up doing the story. Maybe I won't even call my crew out here—but it won't be because someone wants to scare me off. It'll be because I decide to call it quits."

"Whatever you say, Ms. St. Regis." Unger pulled open the door. "Just keep calling us, especially if these pranks start to escalate."

"Escalate?" Beth licked her lips. "It's just a story, just a town's rep."

"You'd be surprised how far people will go to protect what's theirs."

She and Duke ended up following Unger back to the reception desk to switch her room to the second floor—next to Duke's.

Unger scanned the footage while they waited and shook his head. "Nothing out of the ordinary. Anyone coming in or out of that parking lot is accounted for as a guest of the hotel."

Gregory slipped her the new card key. "As I said, Ms. St. Regis, I'll question housekeeping tomorrow morning and we'll try to get to the bottom of how someone got into your room. It won't happen again."

"Damn right it won't."

Duke got that fierce look he must've learned on the mean streets of Philly and Beth shivered. It meant a lot to have a man like Duke on your side—if you weren't stupid enough to throw it all away.

Gregory even looked a little worried. "I'll keep you posted, Ms. St. Regis."

Duke took the suitcase handle from her and dragged her bag toward the elevator.

She shuffled after him, yawning. "I am so ready to call it a night."

Duke gave her a sideways glance and stabbed the button for the second floor. The elevator rumbled into action and Beth closed her eyes. The wine had made her sleepy, and she felt the lure of a comfy bed with no surprises in it, although she wouldn't mind one surprise— a prince instead of a frog.

The elevator lurched to a sharp halt and Beth's eyes flew open. "Whoa. This thing needs service."

The elevator had stopped moving but the doors remained shut.

"Oh, God, not another prank—as Unger called it." Her gaze darted to Duke's face, still fierce but set, his jaw hard.

"I'm the one who stopped the elevator."

"What?" She braced her hand against the wall of the car. "Are you crazy? What did you do that for?"

Duke crossed his arms and widened his stance as if she could pull off an escape from the car.

"You're going to tell me what you're really doing in Timberline, and you're going to tell me now or this elevator isn't going anywhere."

Chapter Six

Duke felt a twinge of guilt in his gut as Beth's pale face blanched even more. Was she claustrophobic, too? He knew she had those panic attacks, and if she started down that road he'd cave. He had a weakness for this woman.

"I...I don't know what you're talking about. I'm here to do a *Cold Case Chronicles* episode on the Timberline Trio—come hell or high water."

"Cut it, Beth. That's not your kind of story and we both know it." He leveled a finger at her. "You're up to something. You may have fooled me two years ago, but I'm tuned in to the Beth St. Regis line of baloney now."

Her eye twitched and her tongue darted from her mouth. "It's personal."

He rolled his shoulders. "Now we're getting somewhere. I knew there was more to this story. Start talking."

"If I do, will you help me?"

He tilted his head back and eyed the ceiling. "Just like you to turn the tables. I'm not agreeing to anything. I just want to know the truth—for a change. Don't you think you owe me the truth?"

Tears brightened her eyes, and the tip of her nose turned red.

He scooped in a deep breath. If she shed even one tear, he'd be finished. But that was how she'd gotten around him last time—pushed all his buttons.

"C'mon, Beth. What are you doing here?"

Drawing in a shaky breath, she covered her eyes with one hand. "You're right. It's not just the Timberline Trio case that brings me here, but in a way it is."

"Is this going to be a guessing game?"

"No." She sniffled. "I do owe you the truth, but do we have to do this here, like I'm some suspect you're interrogating?"

He punched the button. "Sorry about that. I just wanted to get your attention. You're not…?"

"Claustrophobic?" Her lips trembled into a smile. "Sort of."

The doors opened onto the second floor and he ushered her out of the car in front of him and then wheeled her suitcase down the hall after her, his gaze taking in the way the soft flannel draped over her derriere. Beth was probably the only woman he knew who could make flannel pajamas look sexy.

She stopped in front of the room next to his and swiped the card key. As she fumbled with the door, he reached around her and pushed it open.

"You want me to check for frogs in the bed?"

"My tormentor doesn't know my new room number, but go ahead anyway."

In three strides he reached the king-size bed and whipped back the covers. "Frog-free."

She climbed onto the bed and crossed her legs beneath her. "You ready?"

Pulling the chair from the desk in the corner, he straddled it. "I'm always ready for the truth."

"You know I'm adopted."

"And you hit the jackpot with a set of rich parents." He held up his hands. "I know they weren't the best parents, but at least they gave you all the creature comforts your teenage mother couldn't give you."

"I didn't have a teenage mother."

"What?" He hunched over the back of the chair. "You told me your birth mother was an unwed teen who gave you up to a wealthy couple for a better life and then disappeared."

"I lied."

He flinched as if she'd thrown a knife at his heart. What didn't she lie about?

"Okay. Who was your mother and what does this all have to do with Timberline?"

"Duke, I don't know who my birth parents are. My adoptive parents, the Kings, never told me."

"Maybe they didn't want you running after some bio parents and getting disappointed."

She snorted. "I doubt that."

"They wouldn't give you any information? The adoption agency? A birth certificate?"

"I...I think my adoption was illegal. My birth certificate is fraudulent. The Kings are listed as my biological parents. The only reason I even knew I was adopted was because I overheard them talking once. When I confronted them about it, they admitted it but refused to give me any more information."

"That's strange, but what does it all have to do with Timber...?" Her implication smacked him on the back of the head. She couldn't be serious.

"That's right." She dragged a pillow into her lap and

hugged it. "I think I'm one of the Timberline Trio—Heather Brice."

He pushed up from the chair and took a turn around the room. "How in the hell did you come to that conclusion?"

She launched into a crazy tale of stuffed frogs and repressed memories of forests and news stories of Timberline until his head was swimming.

"Wait." He sank onto the edge of the bed. "Based on a stuffed frog you had as a child that happens to be Timberline's mascot, you think you were kidnapped and then what? Sold on the black market?"

"Don't pretend that doesn't happen. We both know it does, and the Kings were just the type to be involved in something like that. The rules didn't apply to them. Their riches always gave them a sense of entitlement."

"From what you've told me about your adoptive parents, I agree. But, Beth…" He reached across the bed and tugged on the hem of her pajama bottoms. "Maybe you have that frog because your parents, the Kings, passed through this area and bought it for you."

"I thought of that, not that I could ever see them vacationing in Timberline, but what about the hypnosis?" She waved her arms in a big circle. "I went to a hypnotist in LA, and I saw this place—the lush forest, the greenery—and it scares the hell out of me."

"There are a lot of places in the world that look like Timberline."

"But combined with the frog?"

"Maybe something traumatic happened here when your parents were passing through. Hell, maybe there was a car accident or you wandered away and got lost—

God knows, you'd be the kind of kid to do that, and I mean that in a good way."

"The Kings never mentioned anything like that."

"Why would they? You said they were distant, uncommunicative."

"I just feel it, Duke." She pounded her chest with one fist. "From the moment I saw the Wyatt Carson story and the Timberline scenery on TV, I felt it in my bones. There's something about this place. I have a connection to it."

"Have you tried to contact the Brices?"

"No. I don't want to get their hopes up or make them think this is some cruel joke. I want to do some legwork first."

"I thought you were convinced you were Heather Brice."

"There's being convinced and then there's proving it. I came here to prove it."

"It would be easy to know for sure with a DNA test."

"I can't put those poor people through that if I'm not sure."

"What do you think is going to happen here? You're going to have some revelation? Everything that happened to you at age two is suddenly going to come back to you in perfect recall?"

She stretched her legs out in front of her and tapped her feet together. "I'm not sure. I just know I have to be here, and I have to investigate."

"You can't go to the Brice house anymore. It's been torn down along with its neighbors to make room for a shopping center."

"I know that." She drew her knees up to her chest

and clasped her arms around her legs. "Does this mean you're going to help me?"

He jerked back. How'd he get sucked in so quickly? He planted his feet on the carpet. Was she even telling the truth now? Maybe it was all a trick to get him to turn over what he knew about the Timberline Trio so she could film her stupid show and maybe even piggyback on his success like last time.

She saw it in his face—the doubt.

She touched her forehead to her knees and her strawberry blond hair created a veil over her face. Her voice came out muffled and unsteady. "I'm not playing you, Duke."

A sharp pain knifed the back of his head. He was done—for now.

"You've had a crazy day. Get to bed and we'll discuss it tomorrow." He pushed off the bed and made it to the door. He yanked it open and paused as she rolled off the bed as if to follow him.

He raised one eyebrow.

"I have to brush my teeth again. Thanks for suggesting this room. I know it's just a frog and a broken window, but I feel better being close to you."

"Good night, Beth."

As the door shut behind him, a whisper floated after him. "I always did feel better close to you."

THE FOLLOWING MORNING Beth opened her eyes and stretched, feeling fifty pounds lighter. There had been a moment at the end of the evening when it looked like Duke was ready to bolt, but overall he'd taken her confession well. And he'd believed her.

She hadn't revealed everything to him, but she wasn't ready for that…and neither was he. Maybe she'd feel another fifty pounds lighter once she did.

Sitting up in bed, she reached for her phone and checked her messages. Scott had asked when she needed her cameraman and the rest of the crew. Maybe she'd never need them. If she played it cool and didn't make a big fuss, her tormentor might stop harassing her and she could get down to the business of her real investigation.

The tap on her door made her yank the covers up to her chin.

"Beth, are you up yet? I talked to the cleaning crew, and I think I know how the intruder got into your hotel room."

"I'm awake. Just a minute." She scrambled out of bed, ran her tongue along her teeth and lunged for the door.

"Sleeping in?"

"I was exhausted." She swung the door wide. "Come on in. What did the maids have to say?"

He put a finger to his lips and closed the door. "Let's not broadcast this. They had a cart on your floor at about the time we figured someone broke into your room. They carry master room keys with them, and Gregory thinks someone walked by and snatched one, letting himself in your room."

"Doesn't say much for their security, does it?"

"What security? But the hotel is going to change its policy, and now each maid will have a single master key— no more leaving them on the carts. I'm not sure they were supposed to be doing that anyway."

"I hope I didn't get anyone in trouble." She ran her fingers through her hair, wishing she'd told Duke to wait until she'd showered and dressed. "Have you had breakfast yet?"

"No. I went for a run and then met with Gregory."

"Wish I'd been able to join you." She glanced at the alarm clock. "Can I buy you breakfast?"

"To continue our discussion from last night?"

"To eat breakfast."

"Pound on the wall when you're ready."

She released a pent-up breath when Duke left. Still testy, but he seemed as if he trusted her a little more after sleeping on her revelation. She'd have to make sure that trust continued to grow. She could use his help... and maybe his protection while unraveling her past.

She showered and dressed for the weather in a pair of jeans, a sweater and the boots she'd been wearing every day since she got here. Before leaving the room, she called the rental-car company to report the broken window.

Instead of banging on the wall, she knocked on Duke's door.

He answered with a file folder in his hand. As he held it up, he said, "You may want to just eat breakfast, but I have to get to work. Yesterday was a wash."

"There's a restaurant a few miles from here that serves breakfast." She averted her eyes from the folder. If he wanted to share with her, he would.

"We'll take my car. Did you call the rental-car place?"

"I just did. They're swapping out the car for me. Seemed so surprised about the vandalism and theft."

"I guess it is unusual for this town unless you're determined to dwell on its ugly past."

"You know what I was thinking?" She ducked into

the stairwell as Duke held the door for her. "I should've come here as a tourist and done my own detective work without the glare of publicity."

"Without bringing the spotlight with you, a lot of those people last night at the restaurant wouldn't have any interest in talking to you about the case. They might've recognized you anyway and had their suspicions. You just didn't realize not everyone would be thrilled with the show coming to town."

"It's not like it hasn't happened before—people unhappy with the show coming to their town." She shoved open the fire door to the lobby. "I'm going to put those pranks out of my mind and concentrate on my goal. Nothing is going to stop me."

She glanced at the front desk on her way out but another clerk had replaced Gregory. When they reached the parking lot, Beth spotted the ex-con she'd run into before, straddling his bike and examining her broken car window.

"That's the guy I saw in the forest." She elbowed Duke and called to the man. "I saw you in the forest."

The man looked up, a green baseball cap low on his forehead. "Is this your car?"

"It's a rental."

"That's a shame." He scratched his chin. "I heard why you were here—from them teenagers drinking in the woods."

"Do you want to get on camera now, too?"

"No, ma'am. Some things are just better off left alone." He got back on his bike and pedaled away.

"Do you know that man was questioned for the Carson kidnappings?"

Duke waved the file at her. "I do. His name is Gary Binder and he's a former junkie and an ex-con."

"Were you going to tell me about him?" She walked to the passenger side and he followed her. "I mentioned him to you yesterday."

As he opened the door, he shrugged. "Would you blame me for keeping my research to myself?"

Before she could answer, he turned and walked back to the driver's side.

By the time Duke got behind the wheel, she'd decided not to push her luck. If Duke wanted to help her in her quest, he'd do it. She wouldn't push him, wouldn't cajole. When she'd started this journey, she'd had no idea that Duke would be here. His presence did give her a sense of comfort, but she was determined to dig into this thing on her own and to discover the truth with or without Duke.

While he drove, she gave him directions to the little café that sat near a creek bed and served breakfast and lunch only. As they entered the restaurant, she pointed to the back. "They have a deck next to a running creek, but it looks like rain."

"I have a feeling it always looks like rain in Timberline, and I don't want my papers floating away."

A waitress shoved through the swinging doors to the kitchen with a row of plates up each arm. "Sit anywhere. I'll be right with you."

They took a corner table and Duke turned his coffee cup upright. "You still drinking decaf tea?"

"You remembered?" For some reason, the fact that he remembered she'd been trying to give up caffeine gave her a warm glow. "I've been to this place already for breakfast and they have a good selection."

The waitress approached with a coffeepot. "Coffee?"

"Just one. Black." Duke inched his cup to the edge of the table.

"I'll have some hot tea, please."

Duke blew the steam rising from his cup. "How much do you know about Heather Brice?"

"She was the youngest kidnap victim at two, and she was snatched from her toddler bed while her babysitter slept on the couch in front of the TV."

"She was also the last of the Timberline Trio."

"The FBI at the time ruled out any connection between the missing children—no babysitters in common, no teachers, no day care, not even any friends, although Kayla Rush and Stevie Carson knew each other."

"You *have* done your homework." He took a sip of coffee as the waitress delivered her hot water and a selection of tea bags.

"One thing I don't know?"

"Yeah?"

"The new evidence. After the Carson kidnap case was resolved, law-enforcement officials mentioned that new evidence about the older case had come to light, but nobody ever mentioned what that evidence was." She tapped the folder on the table between them. "I'm assuming that's what you have here."

"If you're expecting a bombshell, this isn't it. No confessions. No long-lost bloody handprint. No DNA evidence."

"But enough to send an FBI agent out here to take a look at this cold case."

"An FBI agent who doesn't have anything better to do with his career right now."

"I heard about what happened, Duke. I'm sorry you lost your partner."

"But we saved the child. Tony, my partner, wouldn't have wanted it any other way, and I'm not making excuses for our decision. We both went into that warehouse with our eyes wide-open, both knowing the risks. We were willing to take those risks. Believe me, I would've taken that bullet instead of Tony if it meant saving the kid."

"The FBI didn't blame you."

"Not exactly, but look at me now." He spread his arms.

"I'm glad you're here." She dredged her tea bag in the hot water. "Is your boss expecting any results out here?"

"Mick always expects results. The Timberline Trio case has been a black eye for the FBI for twenty-five years."

"Maybe Mickey Tedesco thinks you're the man to repair that."

"Doubt it."

The waitress hovered at the table. "Are you ready to order?"

Duke flipped open the menu. "Haven't even looked."

"I'll go first." Beth poked at the menu. "I'll have the oatmeal with brown sugar, nuts, banana…and do you have any berries?"

"Fresh blueberries."

"That's fine."

Duke ordered some French toast and bacon.

When the waitress left, he wrapped his hands around

his coffee cup. "I don't get why you just don't contact the Brices, tell them your story and get a DNA test done."

"You know about the Brices, right?"

"That they're super wealthy? Yeah, I know that."

"Don't you think they'd be suspicious of people popping out of the woodwork claiming to be their long-lost daughter? It's probably happened to them before."

"You're already rich. You don't need their money."

"I'm hardly in the same league as the Brices. Do you know how much of their wealth my adoptive parents left to charities and foundations, cutting me out?"

"You mentioned that before, but my point is you're not some pauper trying to cash in on the Brices' wealth."

"I couldn't put them through anything like that based on a hunch."

"Now it's a hunch?" He tilted his head. "You were one hundred percent sure last night that you were Heather Brice."

She linked her fingers together. "It just all makes sense. I can't explain it to you. Even if Timberline had never experienced those kidnappings, I would've been drawn to this town. The fact that a little girl went missing twenty-five years ago only adds to my conviction."

"I don't know why I can't reveal the new evidence. It's not top secret." Duke dragged the folder toward him with one finger. "It has to do with drugs—the methamphetamine market, to be exact."

"Drugs?" Her hand jerked and a splash of hot tea sloshed into her saucer. "What would drugs have to do with a trio of kidnappings?"

"That's what I'm here to figure out. At the time of the

kidnappings, law enforcement wasn't looking at other illegal activities in the area. The Timberline Sheriff's Department wasn't forthcoming about the drug trade to the FBI. Who knows why not? These petty jealousies between the local law and the FBI always crop up in cases like this—most of the time to the detriment of solving the case."

"So, the FBI discovered that there was a thriving drug trade in Timberline during the investigation of the recent kidnappings."

"Yep, and we got a lot of our information from Binder, the ex-con on the bike."

"It's not hard to imagine he was involved in drugs. Is that what he went away for?"

"He's been in and out of jail—petty stuff mostly, but what he lacked in quality, he made up for in quantity."

She traced a finger around the base of her water glass. "Are you thinking some sort of human trafficking for drugs?"

"It's a possibility."

Beth shivered. "That's horrible. Why those children?"

"Could've been crimes of opportunity. Those kids were unlucky enough to be in the wrong place at the wrong time. A lot of crime is like that."

"Still not much to go on."

"I told you—Siberia." He planted his elbows on the table. "Now tell me what you think you're going to accomplish. How are you going to figure out if you're Heather?"

She paused as the waitress delivered their food. "Anything else for you?"

Duke held up his cup. "Hit me again?"

"I'm a little embarrassed to admit this, but I thought I might just show up here and it would all come back to me." She swirled a spoonful of brown sugar through her oatmeal without looking up and meeting Duke's eyes, although she could feel his dark gaze drilling her.

"I'm sorry, Beth."

She raised her eyes and blinked. "You are?"

"I'm sorry your parents were so cold and distant. I always thought you had it better than I did with your money and private schools and fancy vacations, but you suffered a form of abuse just as surely as I did."

"I would never compare my life of luxury to what you went through with your father, Duke."

"At least my mom loved me, even though I couldn't save her or my sister from that man."

"Your father and mine were two sides of the same coin, weren't they?"

"And now you're driven to find your real family, but what if this journey doesn't end well?"

"You mean what if I'm not Heather Brice, loved and missed by her family?"

"Can you take the disappointment?"

"Of course." She dug into her oatmeal to hide her confusion. She'd been so convinced she was Heather, she hadn't allowed any doubt in her worldview—until now.

"When do you start your interviews? I can probably get Deputy Unger to talk to you. Maybe if his mom's still in town, she can talk to you about Heather's family."

Beth took a sip of tea to melt the lump in her throat. Only yesterday after she'd sprayed Duke in the face with pepper spray and he'd stalked off had she figured she'd get nothing more from him, and yet here he was, offering to save her again.

Despite his hard shell, he had a soft heart. That was why he thought he could save all the kids of the world.

"I thought…well, I figured you were done helping me with cold cases."

"I don't see this as a *Cold Case Chronicles'* investigation. I see this as a Beth St. Regis investigation."

"I figured you'd be done with that, too."

"Maybe I should be." He bit off the end of a piece of bacon.

"Duke, it was never just about the evidence." She hunched forward. "I don't know how you could've believed that after what we had."

"You used me, Beth—straight-up."

"I took the case files from your room when I spent the night with you, but I didn't spend the night with you to get the case files. How could you think that?"

"Easy. We had sex and then you snuck out in the early morning hours, taking my files with you."

She sighed. If he'd let her prove to him that she wanted him regardless of what he could do to help her, she could convince him in one night.

She dropped her spoon into her bowl as the truth punched her in the gut. She *did* still want Duke Harper, had never stopped wanting him. She just had one more truth to tell him and she didn't know if he'd ever get over that one.

He turned the file toward her. "Do you want to see this or is it just more fun skulking around in my room?"

"I'll take a look."

While Duke polished off the rest of his breakfast, Beth sifted through the pile of papers in the folder. Apparently, Timberline had suffered from a flourishing meth trade as the town's economy tanked. A lot of money exchanged hands and there had been a spike in crime. Could the drug dealers have branched into trafficking? It happened all over the world. Why would a small town in Washington be immune?

She closed the file. "That's some scary stuff."

"You can see it's not a stretch to imagine that druggie bunch might've been into some other serious crimes."

The waitress tucked the bill between the salt and pepper shaker and Beth grabbed it. "I'll use my expense account in exchange for the information. You see? Everything on the up-and-up."

"Sounds fair." Duke stood up and stretched. "I'm going to have a few meetings today with local law enforcement. Are you going to start making calls and setting up interviews with tomorrow's budding TV stars?"

"I suppose I have to start somewhere." She handed her credit card to the waitress. "Who knows? Maybe someone will recognize me as Heather Brice."

She signed the receipt and joined Duke outside. "I hope the rental company replaced my car already."

"I'll drop you off at the hotel." He placed a hand at the small of her back, propelling her toward the car. "Stay alert. Don't leave stuff in your car and make sure nobody's following you."

"Following me?" She hugged herself. "That's creepy. I hadn't thought of that."

"Just watch it. I'll even replace your pepper spray for you."

He started the car and wheeled out of the gravel parking lot of the restaurant.

They'd traveled just a half mile when traffic slowed down and the revolving lights of some emergency vehicles lit up the gray sky.

"Traffic accident?"

Duke craned his neck out the window. "I don't see any cars except the ones on the road."

Beth powered down her own window and stuck her head out. "It's a bike at the side of the road—a twisted bike."

Then she saw it—a gurney with a sheet covering a body…and a green baseball cap on the ground.

Beth's stomach churned and her nails dug into the seat of the car. "Oh, my God. It's Gary Binder and I…I think he's dead."

Chapter Seven

"What?" Duke slammed on the brakes and the car lurched forward and back. "How can you tell?"

"That's his bike up ahead and there's a body on a gurney with a sheet covering the head."

"How do you know it's Binder? Maybe his bike's there because he stopped to help."

"It's the hat—the green baseball cap. It's on the ground next to the stretcher." Beth covered her mouth. "We were just talking to him. Literally, he could've been hit right after he left the parking lot of the hotel."

"We don't even know if he's been hit. I still don't see any cars stopped except for the emergency vehicles and all of us on the road." He swung the SUV onto the shoulder of the road.

"What are you doing?"

"I'm still an officer of the law, and I'm going to find out what happened."

His tires churned up gravel as he hugged the shoulder, rumbling past the cars stuck on the road.

A deputy stepped up to block his progress, so Duke threw the car into Park and grabbed the door handle. Turning to Beth, he said, "Stay here."

When he slammed his car door, he heard an echo from the other side and saw Beth heading toward the crash scene. Did he expect anything different from her?

He caught her arm and whispered, "Let me do the talking."

"Folks, you need to get back in your car and keep moving."

Duke flashed his badge. "Special Agent Harper. I'm here on FBI business, Deputy, and I think the victim here is—was one of my witnesses."

As the deputy squinted at his badge, he said, "Gary Binder. Is that your man?"

Beth stiffened beside him.

Duke said, "That's him. What happened?"

"Hit and run."

Beth grabbed his arm and squeezed hard. "Any witnesses?"

"Not yet. Follow me." The deputy jerked his thumb toward the ambulance. "Damn shame since the guy was finally getting his life together."

Beth kept a grip on Duke as they walked toward the gurney, draped with a white sheet, the outlines of a body beneath it, a bloodstain near the head.

Duke didn't need to see Binder and Beth really didn't need to see him. "Who called the police?"

"Someone on a cell phone in a car. She noticed the bike first, and when she slowed down, she saw Binder's body just off the road."

"Any evidence? Tire tracks? Brake skid marks?"

"Nothing yet, but we're going to let the accident investigators do their thing." The deputy shook his head. "Timberline seems to be losing its civility ever since Evergreen Software went in—too many city folks bringing the hustle and bustle with 'em."

Duke swallowed hard. Was that what you called a hit and run out here? A lack of civility? "Maybe someone will step forward or the driver will have an attack of conscience."

"Do you need anything else from me, Agent Harper? We can forward the accident report to you once it's complete."

"That would be helpful, thanks." He started heading back to the SUV with Beth attached to his arm. Halfway to the car, he turned. "Deputy? What was Binder doing out here on his bike?"

"Not sure. He'd been working as a handyman, doing odd jobs, but as far as I know, most of his work was in town. He always rode that damned bike. Someone had even given him a truck recently, but he stuck with the bike."

"To the very end."

Duke climbed into the car and glanced at Beth, whose wide eyes took up half her face. "Are you okay?"

"That's so…creepy. We were just talking to him." She knotted her fingers in her lap. "What was he doing at the Timberline Hotel?"

"Riding on his way to work or wherever he was going." He drummed his thumbs against the steering wheel. "Maybe he was doing work at the hotel and that's what brought him out this way."

"If he was at the hotel…"

"You're thinking he was the one who broke into your room and left the frog head?"

She nodded. "But why would he do that?"

"He'd do it if he was the one warning you."

"He doesn't have any real estate to worry about. Why would he want to scare me off this story?"

"Maybe he was involved in the Timberline Trio disappearance more than he let on in his interview." He cranked on the engine. "I'm throwing that out there, but I have a hard time believing Gary Binder would be sending anonymous emails to the FBI."

"Do you think his death—a hit and run—is just coincidental to all this other stuff?"

"Maybe, maybe not, but it doesn't have to be related to his involvement in the kidnappings or to the threats against you. Binder's the one who gave the FBI information about the drug trade at the time of the kidnappings."

Beth clasped her fidgeting hands so tightly her knuckles turned white. "You think someone was trying to shut him up?"

"Could be, even though it's a little late. He already spilled, unless…"

"Unless he had more to spill." Her knees began to bounce.

"Maybe that's why he was at the hotel. He knew you were staying there and wanted to talk to you. He didn't want to open up in front of me, so he pretended to be looking at the broken window. I'm going to have to review his previous interview carefully." He pulled into the line of traffic, crawling past the accident site. "But if he had more information, I don't know why he didn't give it up the first time."

"I don't know, Duke, but there seem to be some real forces of evil at work in Timberline."

As they passed the last emergency vehicle, Duke

looked in his rearview mirror just as the ambulance doors closed on Gary Binder's body. A chill touched his spine.

Whatever evil held sway over Timberline, he'd do whatever it took to keep it far away from Beth…even as she ran toward it.

WHEN THEY GOT back to the hotel, the rental-car company had dropped off her replacement car. Duke walked around the car, examining it. He ran his hand along the roof. "Don't leave anything out on your seat this time."

"C'mon, Duke. We both know the vandal would've broken into my car with or without that bag on the seat. He was sending me a message."

"Thanks for the reminder. I'm going to get you a fresh container of pepper spray. At least you proved you know how to use it."

"Are you going to take off for your meetings?"

"After I ask the front desk about Binder. You coming?" Maybe he was stalling, but he didn't want to leave Beth alone. Funny how he'd done a complete one-eighty from yesterday—a few threats could do that.

"Sure, I'll come with you. My interviews can wait."

They walked into the lobby together, and Tammy, the receptionist at the check-in counter, looked up from her computer screen and waved. "Hello. Can I get you anything? I heard about your room, Ms. St. Regis, and we want to make your stay here hassle-free from here on out. The maid staff is being extra careful now."

"I appreciate that."

Duke rested his arms on the counter. "Tammy, do you know a local guy, Gary Binder?"

Her mouth formed an O. "I just heard. He's dead—hit-and-run accident. Who could do that? I never liked Gary much, but you don't leave a dog to die in the street without stopping. Am I right?"

News did travel quickly in Timberline. "Absolutely. I hope they catch the bastard and string him up."

Her eyes popped. "Wh…what did you want to know about Gary?"

"Did the hotel ever hire him to do any work around here?"

"Gary? No way. Management knew his reputation, even though Kendall Rush had given him a chance when she was here."

Beth cleared her throat. "Isn't Kendall Rush the sister of one of the Timberline Trio?"

"Twin." The clerk pulled the corners of her mouth down with two fingers. "She was out here to sell her aunt's house and got caught up with all the craziness with Wyatt Carson. But while she was here, she hired Gary to do some work at the house. I guess he did okay, but management here would still never hire him."

"Do you know why he'd have any reason to be at this hotel? In the parking lot?" Duke tipped his head in that direction. "We saw him out there, probably just before he got hit."

"Really?" Tammy's eyes got even bigger. "I don't know why he'd be here, just passing by, I guess." She licked her lips. "Do you think the sheriff's department is going to want to look at our security tapes of the parking lot?"

"Probably. In fact—" Duke slid his badge across the counter "—I wouldn't mind having a look myself."

"Okay. I know you're FBI and all, but can I call my manager first?"

"Sure." He glanced at Beth. "You can take off if you want, set up those interviews."

"I think I'd rather watch this video." She leaned in close, putting her lips next to his ear, and said in a low voice, "Why do you think Kendall Rush hired him?"

"Don't know. Maybe she felt sorry for him."

Tammy got off the phone. "My manager says it's okay."

She invited them behind the counter and into a small room. She hunched over a set of computer monitors and clicked through several files, launching a video. "This is from earlier today. How long ago did you see him?"

"Over two hours ago."

She cued up the tape, and after several minutes, Gary Binder with his green ball cap came into the frame, walking his bike.

Beth jabbed her finger at the display. "Is he talking to someone out of the picture?"

Binder kept looking over his shoulder, but Duke couldn't see his mouth moving.

"I'm not sure. Maybe he's just watching for cars as he comes into the parking lot, but he seems to have a purpose for coming into the lot."

"Yeah, he's looking at my rental."

After checking behind him once more, Binder wheeled up to Beth's rental car and poked his head inside the broken window. A minute later Duke and Beth appeared in the frame.

They watched a bit longer, but Binder never returned to the parking lot after they took off.

Tammy scrunched up her face. "Looks like he just wanted a closer look at your car."

"Why did he keep glancing over his shoulder? There's not that much traffic on the road." Beth stepped back from the monitors and folded her arms. "Because if there had been, someone would've seen the car that hit him."

"Maybe someone did." Duke backed out of the claustrophobic room. "Thanks, Tammy. I'll tell the sheriff's department about seeing Binder in the parking lot here, and they'll probably want to review that tape, too."

Her fingers flew across the keyboard as she closed down the recordings. "I just wish there was something on there. I suppose they told Gary's mom already. She's a tough, old lady, but Gary was her only kid."

"Sounds like the guy couldn't catch a break." He turned to Beth. "Are you taking off now? I'll be at the sheriff's station if you need me."

"And I'll be setting up shop somewhere to do some interviews."

"You could do them here in your hotel room, or maybe the hotel lobby."

"If I've learned anything from the show, it's that people feel more comfortable talking in their homes."

"Just don't go to Bill Raney's home to interview him." He pushed open the hotel door and they stepped outside.

"I'm not going to be interviewing people who don't want to talk to me."

"How do you know if they're being honest?" He aimed the key fob at his car and the horn blipped. "They could pretend and then change their story when they get you alone."

"I'm only going to talk to the ones I gave cards to

last night—Chloe the waitress and a few senior citizens. You don't think I have anything to fear from them, do you?"

"Be careful, Beth. If the same person who's warning you is the same person who hit Binder, he's just added murder to his résumé."

She rubbed her arms. "If someone did kill Gary, it's because he knew something. I know nothing."

"Not yet and maybe you should keep it that way."

"I'll be careful, Duke." She got behind the wheel of her new rental and pressed her palm against the glass.

He waved back. He had no choice but to leave her.

When he drove past the accident scene, the ambulance had already left with its sad cargo and one cop car remained, directing traffic.

Was Binder's death really connected to his willingness to speak up about the Timberline drug trade twenty-five years ago? Deputy Unger had mentioned tweakers being responsible for the vandalism of Beth's car. Did that mean the drug culture was alive and well in Timberline today?

He hoped all Beth got today was half-baked stories of Wyatt Carson. She didn't need to be involved in this case any more than she already was.

He'd almost been relieved to hear about her ulterior motive for being in Timberline. Maybe once she found out she wasn't Heather Brice, she'd give up on this story.

And if she *was* Heather Brice? What could be the danger in that? She'd leave Timberline, reconnect with her long-lost family who now resided in Connecticut and live happily ever after...or not.

Duke's cop radar gave him an uneasy feeling about

that scenario. What if the Brice family rejected her, too? She talked a tough game, but she had a vulnerable side she tried hard to mask.

He could speed up the entire process by requesting DNA from the Brices as part of this investigation. They wouldn't even have to know about Beth and her suspicions. Once Beth knew the truth—one way or the other—she could stop sleuthing around Timberline.

He pulled up to the sheriff's station and entered the building with a few file folders tucked under his arm. He hadn't met the new sheriff yet, who was probably just getting up to speed.

Deputy Unger greeted him at the desk.

"I'm here to see Sheriff Musgrove."

"The sheriff's expecting you. Go on back, first office on the right."

Duke thanked him and made his way to the sheriff's office. He tapped on the open door and a big man rose from the desk dominating the office.

"Agent Harper? I'm Sheriff Musgrove."

Duke leaned over the desk and shook the sheriff's hand. "Nice to meet you, Sheriff. What do you think of the hit-and-run accident that killed Gary Binder?"

"That's what I like about you fibbies." He smacked his hand against his desk. "Get right to the point. I think Gary Binder was a junkie who was probably riding his bike recklessly on the road, maybe even riding under the influence, if you know what I mean."

Duke studied the man's red face with a sinking feeling in the pit of his stomach. Clearly he had a sheriff on his hands who didn't have the ability to think out of the box. Too bad Sheriff Sloane wasn't still in the position. He'd heard nothing but high praise of Sloane from Agent Maxfield, who'd worked the Wyatt Carson case.

Duke took a deep breath. "You don't find it coincidental that Binder had just given us some information about the Timberline drug trade during the initial kidnappings?"

"The world is filled with coincidences, Harper. I don't find a junkie getting hit by a car all that coincidental."

Duke shoved his hands into his pockets and hunched his shoulders. "By all accounts, Binder was in recovery, hadn't touched drugs in over a year."

"Once a junkie, always a junkie." Musgrove sliced his big hands through the air. "Is that the course you're going to follow on this case, Harper? Are you going to dig up Timberline's sordid past?"

"No town, big or small, is exempt from drugs, Sheriff." Duke narrowed his eyes. "Are you one of the contingents that would rather not have the spotlight on Timberline?"

"Is it a contingent? I'll be damned. I know the town has worked hard to come back from its failures, and we're on the cusp of something great. I plan to work with the mayor and the town fathers to get it there."

Duke's gaze tracked over the sheriff's head to the awards and commendations on the wall, illustrating a career bouncing from agency to agency. He knew law-enforcement types like this guy, scrambling to secure the highest pension with the least amount of work, kissing ass along the way.

He'd have to report back to Mick that Sheriff Musgrove would be more of a hindrance than a help for this cold case.

His eyes dropped to the sheriff's face. "You weren't here during the Carson copycat kidnappings, were you?"

"No, I was over in Spokane. I read about it, though. Crazy SOB. I was hired in after Sheriff Sloane left for Phoenix—took off with that sister of one of the Timberline Trio. Talk about getting wrapped up in the job." He shook his head.

Musgrove would never be one to get too wrapped up in the work. Put in the hours and go home. Duke never understood guys like that.

For him, the work was a calling, a duty. It had been like that for his partner, Tony DeLuca, too. Guys on the other side never got it.

"I understand Sheriff Sloane's daughter was the final kidnap victim."

"Yeah, yeah. Tough break. I guess he couldn't handle it." Musgrove puffed out his chest as if he could handle anything. "Deputy Unger was here for the copycat kidnappings and sat in on the interview with Binder. He's out front if you want to talk to him. Otherwise, you have free rein here, Agent Harper. Our files are your files, and we'll get you that accident report on Binder if you're interested."

"I am. Thanks, Sheriff Musgrove."

They shook hands again and Musgrove sank heavily behind his desk and returned to his computer. Duke didn't have a clue what the man was looking at, but he could guarantee it wasn't work related.

Duke sauntered up front and stopped at Unger's desk.

"Can I ask you a few questions about Gary Binder and the whole Wyatt Carson case?"

"Sure." Unger glanced over his shoulder. "Maybe we can do this over coffee."

Duke got the hint.

"Sheriff Musgrove, Agent Harper and I are going out for coffee to discuss the Binder interview."

The sheriff called from his office. "Did you get those reports done yet?"

"Been on your desk for two hours, sir." Unger rolled his eyes at Duke.

The sound of shuffling papers came from the office. "Got 'em. Keep me posted, Deputy."

"I'll do that, sir."

When they stepped out of the station, Unger tilted his head from side to side, as if cracking his neck.

"The guy's a pain, huh?"

"I'm not gonna bad-mouth my superior, but he's no Coop Sloane."

"I heard good things about Sloane from Agent Maxfield."

"That just proves how good he was, since he and Maxfield didn't always see eye to eye."

"That happens a lot between the FBI and local law enforcement. It's a testament to both of them that they were able to work together and nail Carson."

They'd walked half a block and Unger pointed ahead. "Buy you a coffee?"

"Sure."

A couple of people on laptops huddled at tables and an older gentleman looked up from his paperback when they walked in.

Duke and Unger ordered their coffee and sat across from each other at a table by the window.

Duke stretched out his legs and popped the lid off his cup. "What do you think about Binder's death?"

"I think it's damned strange." Unger took a sip from his cup. "I overheard Musgrove and he's just wrong about Binder. Whatever the guy was into in his past life, he was clean and sober in this one."

"Do you think someone targeted him for his revelations about the Timberline drug trade twenty-five years ago?"

"Seems pointless, doesn't it? We already interviewed him and he told us everything he knew. No point in killing him now."

"Unless he didn't tell you everything. Maybe there was more to come and someone wanted to make sure he kept his mouth shut."

"The thought did cross my mind." Unger tugged on his earlobe. "It's funny that it happened after you showed up and after that TV host came to town."

Duke's pulse jumped. "What do you know about reaction to *Cold Case Chronicles* delving into the Timberline Trio case?"

"It's divided. You have one faction who wants their fifteen minutes of fame and another that's worried about the town's rep and doesn't want this case being rehashed every five years. Most folks want to move on. The families aren't even here anymore."

"Do you think Beth St. Regis is in any danger?"

"Honestly, if she wants my advice, it's not worth it. I don't think the current residents of Timberline are going to be able to give her any juicy new info about the case.

She should find herself another one. I've watched that show before, and she can do a lot better than this."

"Yeah, I've been telling her to move on to something else, but the woman is stubborn."

Especially since she thought Timberline was the key to her past. Duke was still considering ordering DNA from the Brices just to settle this thing for Beth one way or the other.

In fact, that idea was sounding better and better.

Because as much as he wanted Beth right here in Timberline by his side, he had a cold dread that something bad was on the horizon.

Chapter Eight

Beth positioned her video camera on the tripod and smiled at Gail and Nancy. "Could you just start by saying your names?"

Gail jabbed a finger toward the camera. "Does this mean we're going to be on TV?"

Beth gritted her teeth behind her smile. "We shoot a lot of footage, Gail. If we can use it for the story, we'll put it on the show."

She patted her gray perm and smiled. "I'm Gail Fitzsimmons."

Leaning into Gail's space, Nancy said, "And I'm Nancy Heck."

"You don't need to lean over, Nancy. The camera is capturing both of you." Beth cleared her throat. "Did you both know the victims' families?"

Gail answered first. "My daughter used to babysit the twins sometimes."

Beth's heart banged against her rib cage. "Did she babysit Heather Brice, too?"

"Heather was too young. My daughter was seventeen at the time and wasn't interested in sitting toddlers or babies. Kayla and Kendall were older—five-year-olds—potty trained, talking."

"She wasn't babysitting them the night Kayla was kidnapped, though."

"Thank God, no. The parents had left the girls with their aunt. I don't know why. Cass was always a little scatterbrained. Don't you think so, Nancy?"

"Oh, yes, scatterbrained." Nancy seemed transfixed by the camera.

"Is Wendy Simons's family still here?" Beth scribbled on the pad of paper in front of her.

"The girl who was babysitting Heather Brice?" Gail cocked her head at Nancy. "I don't think so. Any of the Simons family around, Nancy?"

"They had a lot of children in that family. That's why Wendy would babysit the little ones. She was the second oldest in her family and helped her mother with her younger siblings."

"I know that, but are any of them still around? That's what Beth's asking."

Nancy reddened to the roots of her silver hair. "I...I don't know about that. I don't think so."

"What was the speculation at the time of the kidnappings?" Beth directed her question to Gail because she was clearly the ringleader and had probably just frightened Nancy into permanent silence.

"With the first one, Kayla, the police actually thought it was the father for a while." Gail affected a stage whisper. "The parents were having troubles."

"But once Stevie Carson was kidnapped, they realized it was something more...more sinister." Nancy placed both hands over her heart.

Gail rolled her eyes at the camera. "I don't know about you, but a father kidnapping or killing his own child is pretty sinister."

"Gail Fitzsimmons, I didn't say it wasn't. Why do you have to twist my words?"

"I understood what she meant, Gail." Beth waved her hands. "Were there any troubles in Stevie's family…or Heather's?"

Nancy had regained her composure and some confidence. "There were always problems in Stevie's family. Maybe that's why Wyatt turned out like he did. But Heather's family? Perfect."

Beth's gaze darted to Gail, waiting for her to disagree with her friend.

But she nodded with a smile on her face. "The Brices were a perfect family, weren't they? The parents adored each other and their children. It was lovely to see and so sad…after."

Beth's nose stung. A perfect family who adored their kids—just the kind of family she'd always dreamed of.

"Yoo-hoo, Beth?"

She snapped out of her daydream. "Yes, go on."

"Do you have any more questions? Because we have a lot more where that came from."

The ladies hadn't told her much she didn't already know, but she could sit and listen to stories about the perfect Brice family all day.

She continued with Gail and Nancy for another forty-five minutes. She'd gotten some colorful quotations from them she might be able to use in the story, but their answers hadn't done much to clear up the mystery—or to solidify her belief that she was Heather Brice.

Beth ended the interview and Nancy sent her away with a tin of cookies and an implied promise of more if their faces wound up on TV. She sent Duke a quick text to let him know where she was, since he'd seemed so concerned when she'd left.

She didn't mind one bit.

Munching on a snickerdoodle, Beth drove to her next appointment at Chloe Rayman's apartment in a new development near the Evergreen Software headquarters. She brought the cookies with her to Chloe's door.

Chloe opened at her knock in full makeup, the ruffle at her low neckline fluttering. "Hello. I'm ready for my close-up, as they say."

"Well, then, let's get set up." She stuck out the tin. "Cookie? They're from Nancy Heck."

"Nancy's famous for her snickerdoodles, but I'll pass. I just brushed my teeth."

Probably flossed and whitened while she was at it.

Beth set up the camera on the tripod and sat in a chair across from Chloe on the sofa. "State your name, please."

"Chloe Rayman. Six eighty-two Treeline Boulevard, number five, Timberline, Washington." She clapped a hand over her lipsticked mouth. "Maybe I shouldn't put all of my personal information out there on TV."

"We'll…ah…edit that out." Beth crossed her legs and took a deep breath. This was gonna be a long interview.

For the next half hour Beth allowed Chloe to chatter on about Wyatt Carson. She had very little insight into the man or what made him tick, and he hadn't talked to her about his brother at all. The interview was worthless to the show and worthless to Beth's personal quest.

As she was trying to think of a way to cut things

short, a knock on the door had Chloe gasping and jumping from the sofa.

"That's my boyfriend, Jason. He's really jealous, so I don't want him to know I've been talking about Wyatt."

"Of course." Beth turned off the camera. "I think I got everything I needed."

Chloe ran to get the door as Beth collapsed the tripod and shoved her notebook into her bag. She glanced over her shoulder as a compact man swept Chloe into a big hug. She met his gaze across the room and he released his girlfriend.

"Sorry. I didn't know you had company."

Chloe waved her hand toward Beth. "This is Beth St. Regis with that *Cold Case Chronicles* show. When she found out I used to know Wyatt Carson, she practically begged to interview me. Beth, this is my boyfriend, Jason Foster."

Jason tucked his shoulder-length dark hair behind one ear. "Hey, Beth."

"Nice to meet you, Jason. I was just leaving." She held out the tin. "Cookie?"

"Thanks." He took the tin from her and popped the lid. "You interviewed Nancy Heck."

"Her snickerdoodles have quite a reputation."

He took a bite of a cookie and brushed some crumbs from his chin. "You have a lot of people up in arms over this story."

"Are you one of them?"

He shrugged. "Doesn't bother me, but the elders are buzzing."

"Elders?" She hitched her bag over one shoulder.

"Jason's Quileute and they're kind of hinky about the Timberline Trio case."

"I met a teenage boy in the woods who told me the same thing. What is it about the case?"

"You got me." He pointed to the tin he'd placed on Chloe's coffee table. "Can I have another cookie?"

"Sure. I suppose anyone who did know wouldn't be willing to talk to me about it."

"Probably not, at least not the old folks."

"And the young folks, like you, probably don't know why it's a taboo topic."

"I sure as hell don't, but my cousin might have a clue." He brushed his hands together. "She's a shaman for the tribe, so certain customs and beliefs have been handed down to her more than the rest of us."

"Does she live in Timberline?"

"Yeah, and she happens to be in town. She travels a lot for her shows."

"Shows?"

Chloe curled her arm around Jason's waist. "Scarlett's an artist, has art shows all over the world."

"That's impressive." Beth's skin had begun to tingle with excitement. A shaman? Someone who knew about the case? Maybe she could help Beth with her own personal agenda.

"Do you think your cousin…?"

"Scarlett. Scarlett Easton."

"Do you think Scarlett would be willing to talk to me?"

"Probably. Her studio's out past the north side of town. You can tell her I sent you."

"Would you mind giving me her number?"

Jason pulled a wallet from his back pocket. "I think I have one of her cards. She only has a cell phone and reception isn't great out there, but you can give it a try."

He fanned out several cards between his fingers and plucked one from the bunch. "Here it is."

Beth scanned the black card with a reprint of a watercolor nature scene splashed on the front. "If this is her work, it's beautiful."

"Yeah, that's one of her more normal works. She does landscapes and then some freaky modern art—that's the stuff that gets her the shows and some big money. You couldn't pay me to hang some of that stuff in my living room."

"Don't tell Scarlett that." Chloe poked Jason's heavily tattooed arm.

Beth held up the card. "Thanks, Jason. In case I can't reach her by phone, can you give me directions to her place?"

"Chloe, do you have paper and a pen?"

"Will the back of an envelope work?" She took two steps toward her small kitchen and grabbed an envelope and pen from the counter, which she handed to Jason.

He squatted down next to the coffee table and sketched out a map. "Scarlett got all the artistic talent in our family, but if you head this way off the main road, you'll see an access road next to a mailbox that's all painted. Follow that and you'll run into Scarlett's place."

Looking at the map, Beth wrinkled her nose. "Do I need four-wheel drive to get there?"

"Nah, it's remote but the access road to the cabin is gravel."

Beth tucked the makeshift map in her back pocket.

"Do you guys want the cookies or maybe I should bring them to Scarlett?"

"We'll take 'em." Jason grabbed the tin and hugged it to his chest. "Scarlett's a vegan or vegetarian or something and doesn't touch the stuff."

"I think you're exaggerating to get cookies." Chloe rolled her eyes at Beth.

"You can keep them anyway." Beth hitched the tripod beneath her arm. "Thanks for your time, Chloe."

Jason got the door for her. "Can I help you carry anything to your car?"

"I got it, thanks."

Beth loaded up the car and, seated in the driver's seat, pulled out her phone. She tapped in Scarlett's number and it went straight to voice mail.

"Scarlett, my name is Beth St. Regis. I'm the host of *Cold Case Chronicles*, and I'm in town to do a story about the Timberline Trio. Your cousin Jason Foster told me you might be able to give me some insight into the Quileute view of the crime. Would love to talk to you."

Beth left her number and checked her texts. Nothing from Duke. He must still be busy with the sheriff's department.

She'd give Scarlett an hour or so to get back to her and then maybe she'd head out to her place in case Scarlett never got her message.

She decided to try Sutter's again for lunch and brought her laptop into the restaurant with her.

The place buzzed with a lunch crowd from Evergreen Software, by the looks of their khakis, pocket protectors and firm grips on their electronic devices.

Beth flagged down the hostess. "Can I get a table for one?"

"Your best bet is a seat at the bar. We serve a full lunch menu at the bar."

"Perfect." Beth hoisted her laptop case over her shoulder and wended her way through the tables to the bar. Heck, she fit right in with her laptop.

She hopped up on a stool and opened her case. As she pulled out her laptop, the bartender placed a menu to the side of it.

"Are you ordering lunch?"

"Yes, and I'll have a cup of hot tea."

"Coming right up." The bartender ducked beneath the counter and clinked a mug on the mahogany bar. "You know Bill Raney wasn't serious about those threats, right?"

Beth focused on the woman's face and realized she'd been tending bar last night when Duke had confronted the loudmouthed Raney.

"Did I think he really wanted to tar and feather me? No. What's your name?"

"Serena Hopewell. And, no, I wasn't here twenty-five years ago." She poured a stream of hot water into Beth's cup.

"Why are you coming to Bill's defense, Serena?"

She shrugged. "He's been having a tough time lately. He's been drinking at this bar way too much. The cops questioned him about a few things this morning, and he doesn't need any more trouble."

"I didn't accuse Bill of anything, but I had a couple of…incidents and his name came up with the deputies." She dunked her tea bag in the water. "They were probably just following up. I don't think he's suspect number one."

"It was enough to get him in trouble with his wife, but that doesn't take much these days." Serena tapped the menu. "Do you need a few minutes?"

"Yeah." As Beth flipped open the menu, someone nudged her shoulder.

"I thought you were going out to Scarlett's place." Chloe's high-pitched voice carried halfway around the restaurant as several people craned their necks to take in the bar.

Beth gave her a tight smile. "Thought I'd have some lunch first, and I did leave her a message."

"Good luck with that. Scarlett likes to keep to herself when she's in town."

Jason came up behind his girlfriend. "Our table's ready. Oh, hey, Beth. Any luck with my cuz yet?"

"Left her a message, will probably pay her a visit this afternoon."

"That's probably the best way to get her attention." He took Chloe's hand. "C'mon, babe. We got a table in Austin's section."

When Beth looked up from her menu, she met Serena's eyes.

The bartender lifted one eyebrow. "You've been busy."

"It's my job. I'm here to work." She closed the menu and held it out. "I'd like the soup-and-sandwich combo— veggie chili and grilled chicken."

"You got it."

Beth flipped up her laptop and checked email. She answered an inquiry about a previous story, replied to an anxious message from Scott and opened a document to take some notes about the two interviews today.

When her lunch arrived, she checked her phone again. Nothing from Scarlett and nothing from Duke.

She took a bite of her sandwich, her teeth crunching through the grilled sourdough. Ever since Jason had told her about his cousin's extrasensory abilities, Beth's mind had been toying with a plan.

She'd seen a hypnotist a few times to try to uncover buried memories about her past. That was where she'd seen visions of the forest, which had evoked such cold terror. But she'd gotten no further with the hypnotist. Someone like Scarlett Easton might be able to help her uncover even more. She had to try…if Scarlett was willing.

She finished her lunch, and as she was slipping her laptop back into its case, a man took the bar stool next to hers.

"Give me that River IPA, Serena."

Beth slid a gaze to her left and Jordan Young caught her eye.

"Hello there, Ms. St. Regis. How's your story going?"

"It's going."

Serena put the beer in front of Young. "Little early in the day for alcohol, isn't it?"

"Rough morning, sweetheart." He raised the glass to Serena and took a sip. "I feel like I need to make up for my friend Bill's boorish behavior, Ms. St. Regis. I'd be happy to talk to you about the Timberline Trio case sometime. I was here—" he patted the top of his head "—with a little more hair."

"I'd be interested in what you have to say, and you can call me Beth."

"Pretty name. And you can call me Jordan."

"Thanks, Jordan."

She slipped off the stool just as Serena hunched toward Jordan. "What do you think about the hit and run that killed Gary?"

Beth didn't get a chance to hear what Jordan thought about Gary as she headed for the door, anxious to meet with Scarlett now that she'd decided on a plan.

When she got to her rental car, she checked all the doors and windows—nothing today. She loaded her laptop in the trunk and pulled Jason's map from her pocket.

When she sat behind the wheel, she flattened the envelope on her thigh and memorized the first few directions.

She made the turn from the main road and passed several houses and access roads until she reached the one with the mailbox painted with chickens. Why chickens?

She turned her rental onto the access road, her tires crunching the gravel and her car rocking back and forth. She drove into a tunnel of trees, feeling the chill as her world darkened.

Suddenly the road ended, but she did see the peak of a roof beyond the tree line. She would've needed a four-wheel-drive vehicle to get close to Scarlett's cabin, but the road had ended within walking distance and a path cut through the trees.

She got out of the car and slammed the door behind her. She glanced at the trunk, where she'd stashed her laptop. Duke had warned her about leaving her stuff in the car, but at least it was out of sight. Who would be out here in the middle of the woods, anyway?

Tugging on her down vest, she headed toward the cabin, her boots crunching through the underbrush.

She took one big step over a fallen log. As something whizzed past her ear, she heard a crack in the distance. She yelled, "Hey," as she fell to the forest floor on her hands and knees.

That was a gunshot—and she was the target.

Chapter Nine

Duke heard the report of a rifle from his open window. Beth could be out there.

He stepped on the gas pedal of his SUV and the car tore across the road, spewing gravel in its wake.

He almost plowed into the back of Beth's car. He lurched to a stop behind the rental and bolted from the car.

"Beth?"

"I'm here. Be careful. Some idiot is shooting a rifle."

"Are you okay?"

"I'm on the ground about twenty feet in front of my car."

Duke hunched forward in case the hunter—or whoever it was—decided to squeeze off any more shots.

He spotted Beth, still crouched on the ground, her eyes wide and her face pale.

"I yelled when I heard the shot and dropped to the ground. I recognized it right away, of course."

"Did you see anything? A hunter? I know it's hunting season right now."

"What the hell is going on?" A woman's voice floated out from the cabin.

Duke cupped a hand around his mouth. "Someone's taking shots out here."

She called back. "Everyone okay?"

"Yes." Beth started to rise. "Do you think it's safe?"

"Even those idiot hunters should know by now we're humans and not some defenseless beast."

Duke reached Beth's side and helped her to her feet.

She grabbed his arm for support. "What are you doing here?"

"Stopped by Sutter's and Jason told me you were planning to see his cousin this afternoon." With his arm around her, he led her to a small clearing where a woman with long, black hair stood in front of a rustic cabin, her hands wedged on her hips.

"And who the hell are you two?"

"Are you Scarlett Easton?" Beth brushed off the knees of her jeans and pushed her hair from her face.

"Who wants to know?" The woman stood even taller, as if challenging them to take one more step.

"I'm Beth St. Regis. Your cousin Jason gave me your number. I tried calling, and I left a voice mail but Jason said you don't always get reception out here."

The woman tossed back her head, and her mane of black hair flipped over one shoulder. "I'm Scarlett Easton, and I don't know why my cousin seems to think I need company, but since some moron almost shot you on my property, come on in."

They followed Scarlett to a wide, wooden porch, almost a deck, and Duke stomped his boots on the first step. "I'm Duke Harper. Does that happen a lot with hunters? Potshots in the forest?"

As Scarlett pushed open her front door, she tilted her head. "Happens a lot around here."

Duke exchanged a glance with Beth as they followed Scarlett into her place. Did that mean the shot wasn't meant for Beth?

Scarlett Easton didn't seem like good interview material for Beth, and it didn't seem as if she wanted anyone on her property. So why had Beth come here?

Beth pointed to a cell phone on a table that had been carved from a tree stump. "Are you going to call the sheriff's department?"

"Reception isn't good today." Scarlett dipped to pick up her phone. "If I didn't get your call, what makes you think I can get a call out to the cops?"

Duke tried his own phone and received a No Service message. "She's right."

"But if you could tell that idiot Sheriff Musgrove someone was shooting a rifle, too close to the road, I'd appreciate it."

Duke dragged a hand across his mouth, wiping away his smile. She had Musgrove pegged already and he hadn't been on the job even two months.

"Can I get you something? Water? Soda? Stiff shot of whiskey?" Scarlett jerked her chin toward Beth. "You look as white as a sheet."

"Maybe some water." Beth placed her hands on her cheeks. "That bullet flew right past my ear."

"Idiots." Scarlett shook her head and asked Duke, "Anything for you?"

"No, thanks."

Scarlett cranked on the faucet in the kitchen and

filled a glass with water. "The stuff from the tap is actually better than the bottled stuff. Ice?"

"Just the water."

Scarlett handed the glass to Beth. "So what brought you to my doorstep? You friends with Jason?"

"I just met Jason today." Beth took a gulp of water, and her gaze darted to Duke's face. "I host a television show called *Cold Case Chronicles*."

"Never heard of it."

Duke scanned the decor of the cabin—a mix of hand-carved furniture, Native American crafts and original artwork—an explosion of colors and textures that overwhelmed the senses. A bookshelf took up one wall and hardback books and paperbacks jockeyed for space on the crammed shelves...but no TV.

Beth took a deep breath. "It's a reality TV show where we investigate cold cases."

"Let me guess." Scarlett raised her eyes to the beamed ceiling. "You're doing a story on the Timberline Trio."

Beth licked her lips. "Jason told me the Quileute are suspicious about the case. He told me you would have some insight into that."

"Jason thought I'd be willing to sit down with a reality TV show and discuss our Quileute heritage?" She snorted, the nostrils of her delicate nose flaring. "He must be smoking the good stuff these days."

Duke watched Beth, uncharacteristically hesitant. She should be halfway to convincing Scarlett an interview would be the best thing that ever happened to her. There had to be something more to this visit to Scarlett.

"I understand that." The glass of water Beth brought to her lips trembled. "That's not really why I'm here."

Duke's eyebrows shot up. "It's not?"

"It's not?" Scarlett echoed him.

"Can we sit down?" Beth hovered near a curved love seat.

"All right." Scarlett grabbed what looked like a hand-painted pillow and dropped into a chair, dragging the pillow into her lap. "Just let me warn you. I'm not doing anything related to some reality TV show, and I'm not exploiting my tribe's traditions and customs."

Normally, Duke would perch on the arm of a chair but didn't want to destroy anything in this room and end up paying thousands of dollars to replace it. He sat on the edge of the love seat, next to Beth.

"What I'm going to ask you has nothing to do with the show. It's about me."

"Let's hear it." Scarlett tapped the pointed toe of her cowboy boot.

Beth squared her shoulders. "I have a mysterious past. I was adopted, but my adoptive parents refused to tell me where I came from, and my birth certificate has their names as my biological parents."

"Go on." Scarlett drew her dark brows over her nose.

"Anyway, I tried hypnosis a few times to try to reveal any memories, but all I got was a cold terror associated with the vision of a forest."

Duke folded his arms over a niggling fear in his chest. Beth wanted Scarlett Easton to perform some ritual mumbo jumbo on her.

Scarlett held up one finger. "Hypnosis can really only work with the memories that are already there. I doubt you have any memories of being a baby."

"That's my problem. Even if I could dig up my earliest memories, they're not going to tell me who I am or where I came from."

"Right. So, what are you doing in Timberline? I'm known as an artist, not a Quileute shaman. You didn't come here for me."

Duke held his breath and tried to catch Beth's eye, but she'd started down a path and there was no turning back.

"I think I'm Heather Brice."

Scarlett whistled. "Are you kidding me?"

"A variety of sources led me to Timberline—that Pacific Chorus frog, the scenery and my response to it, and the missing children. I just feel it."

"Tell me all of it." Scarlett shoved off the chair. "But I need to get comfortable first. Duke, do you want something to drink? A beer? A shot of whiskey?"

"Whiskey? Ah, no, but I'll take a beer. I have a feeling I'm gonna need it."

Scarlett went into the kitchen, her long hair waving down her back. She returned with a bottle of beer, which she handed to him, and her arm around a bottle of whiskey with her index finger and thumb pinching two shot glasses together. She put them on the tree table, filled each one about halfway with the amber liquid and then gave one to Beth.

"Tell me everything." Scarlett held up her shot glass and Beth touched it with hers.

They both downed the whiskey in one gulp.

Beth launched into her story—the same one she'd told him, except she hadn't mentioned the hypnotherapy.

Scarlett interrupted her here and there to ask a question or inject a comment. She was seriously considering helping Beth.

"You don't still have the original frog, do you?"

"No. I remember having that frog as a child and it's in my earliest pictures, but I don't know what my parents did with it. They probably threw it away."

"Do you have anything else from that time period?"

Beth nodded. "A locket."

Duke jerked his head to the side. That was news to him. She'd never told him about that, but then, their relationship hadn't progressed to the stage where they'd known everything about each other.

He'd broken it off when he discovered he couldn't trust her, but now he was beginning to see why Beth might've found it difficult to be completely open with anyone.

"You're sure the locket is from the time before your adoption?"

"I always had it. It's not the kind of thing you'd give to a toddler and it's not something the Kings, my adoptive parents, would've ever given to me."

"They didn't discuss the locket with you?"

"My mother just told me it was mine and that someone had given it to me when I was a baby."

"Do you have it with you?"

"It's in my hotel room. Is it important?"

"What is it you're asking me to do, Beth?"

"I want you to use your…sensitivity to help me confirm that I'm Heather Brice. Can you do that?"

"There are certain rituals I can perform. It might not be pleasant."

"For me? I can handle it."

"For me." Scarlett tipped another splash of whiskey into her glass and tossed it back. "You're not going to be seeing into your past. *I'm* going to be seeing into your past."

Duke felt Beth stiffen beside him. "I can't ask you to do that, not if it's going to bring any harm to you."

"I didn't say it would hurt me. It's just not the most comfortable feeling in the world."

Duke hunched forward, elbows on his knees. "What do you get out of it? Money?"

Scarlett whipped her head around, dark eyes blazing. "I don't do this for money. Do you think I'm back on the rez doing magic tricks for the white man?"

Duke held up his hands. "Just trying to figure out why you'd put yourself out for a stranger."

Scarlett collected her hair in a ponytail and wrapped it around her hand. "Let's just say I have my own reasons."

"Is it true what Jason said about the Quileute being skittish about this case? I heard it from a teenage boy in the woods, too."

"Yes."

"Can I ask why?"

"There's a Quileute legend about the Dask'iya, or basket lady, who steals children in the middle of the night without a trace—and eats them. After the kidnappings, most of the elders were convinced Dask'iya had come back and was responsible for the kidnappings."

"But none of the kidnapped children were Native American."

"Didn't matter. The thought of Dask'iya's return

struck terror in the hearts of the old folks." Scarlett bit the tip of her finger.

"But?" Duke swirled his beer in the bottle. "You think there's more to it?"

"I'm not sure why that fear led to such secretiveness in our community at the time of the kidnappings."

"You think the fear had its basis in something more... earthly?"

"You could say that." Scarlett stretched her arms in front of her. "If we decide to do this, Beth, I'm going to need that locket. By the way, is there anything in the locket? No baby pictures?"

"Hair."

"As in—" Scarlett wrapped a lock of dark hair around her finger "—this?"

"On one side of the locket, there's a lock of blond hair, and on the other side, there's a lock of reddish hair." Beth shook her head so that her strawberry blond hair danced around her shoulders. "Like this."

"Yours and someone else's."

"I guess so. Are you sure you want to do this, Scarlett?"

"Like I said, I have my own reasons, but you can do something for me."

"Name it."

"You and Mr. FBI Agent here can report that gunshot when you go back to town."

One corner of Duke's mouth tilted up. "How'd you know I was FBI?"

"I heard you were coming. I'm not quite the complete recluse that my family thinks I am, and Cody Unger's a friend of mine—you know, Deputy Unger."

"Good man."

"Anyway, I figure the word of an FBI agent might carry more weight than the word of a flaky artist who complains about the hunters all the time."

Beth collected the shot glasses and bottle of whiskey and rose from the love seat. "We would've reported that shot anyway since it almost hit me. Is there anything else we can do?"

"I'll think about it. You think about it, too, Beth. Think about it long and hard… You might not like what you discover."

BY THE TIME they returned to town, reported the shot in the woods and drove into the parking lot of their hotel, a light rain had begun to fall.

Duke unfurled an umbrella he had in his backseat and held it over her head as they dashed for the hotel entrance.

Duke's father may have been an abusive alcoholic, but Duke had learned chivalry from somewhere. Must've been his military training. Beth had been attracted to Duke immediately when she'd met him two years ago. But he'd been a man who'd demanded complete openness and she'd found it increasingly hard to deliver.

Maybe she'd stolen those files from his room to sabotage their relationship and growing closeness. Would she make the same mistake today? Would she even have a chance to make the same mistake?

Duke hadn't changed. Had *she*?

A blaze in the lobby fireplace warmed the room and created a welcoming ambience.

Gregory waved from behind the counter. "We have

our complimentary spiced cider tonight—spiked and unspiked."

Beth headed for the cart next to the fireplace, calling over her shoulder, "If I grabbed a spiked cider after that shot of whiskey at Scarlett's, would you peg me as a lush?"

"Absolutely not as long as you don't judge me." Duke nodded at a couple sharing the sofa in front of the fire. "Mind if we join you?"

The man held up his cup. "The cider's good and not too strong."

Beth picked up two cups of cider from the tray and sank into the chair next to Duke's. "Here you go."

He took the cup from her and placed it on the table between them. "Good fishing today?"

The older man on the sofa glanced up. "How'd you know I was a fisherman?"

"You have the look."

"You mean the look of a fanatic?" The man's wife laughed.

"A dedicated sportsman. How about it? A good haul?"

"Decent."

"Do you hunt, also?"

Beth sat up straighter and watched Duke over the rim of her cup. As Scarlett suspected, Sheriff Musgrove had brushed off the shot in the woods. Deputy Unger indicated that it was protocol to post a notice to all hunters to stay in the areas designated for hunting.

"I've done some hunting, but not this trip." He half rose from the sofa and extended his hand to Duke. "Walt Carver, by the way, and this is my wife, Sue."

"I'm Duke Harper and this is Beth St. Regis."

Holding her breath, Beth waved, but neither Walt nor Sue showed a flicker of recognition. Must not be big reality TV fans.

"Why are you asking? Are you a hunter, Duke?"

"No, but my… Beth almost got hit by a stray bullet from a hunter."

Sue covered her mouth. "That's frightening. That's why I'm glad Walt gave it up."

"Some of these people don't follow the rules and accidents happen."

"How common are accidental shootings?" Duke blew on the surface of his cider before taking a sip.

"I don't have any statistics, but it happens." He patted his wife's knee. "I was always very careful, Sue. No need to worry."

Sue yawned. "For some reason, fishing all day makes me tired. I don't even know if I can muster enough energy to go out to dinner."

"We can order in." Walt took Sue's cup and placed them on the tray. "Nice to meet you folks. Will you be here long?"

"Not sure." Beth smiled. That depended on one beautiful shaman with an attitude.

They said good-night to the other couple and Duke moved to the sofa and stared into the fire, now a crackling orange-and-red blaze.

"What are you thinking?" She settled next to him.

"Wondering if that shot was an accident or intended for you."

"Scarlett seemed to think it had something to do with her." She held one hand to the fire, soaking up its warmth. "The sheriff indicated she called a lot to complain about the hunters and has even started a petition to push their hunting grounds farther north. She doesn't like the hunters and they don't like her."

Duke scratched his chin. "There have been other incidents at her place, but I don't like this, Beth."

"I don't like it, either, but I'm so close." She pinched her thumb and forefinger together. "With Scarlett's help I might finally discover who I am, where I came from."

"And like some fairy tale, you think your mother and father are going to be the good king and queen?"

"I'm prepared for anything, Duke."

"Are you?" He tapped his cup. "If someone could tell you tomorrow whether or not you're Heather Brice, would you leave Timberline?"

"If I *was* Heather, I'd contact the Brices immediately and arrange to see them in Connecticut—if they wanted to see me."

"If you're *not* Heather Brice?"

"I...I'd be back to the drawing board and I'd start following a different path." She leaned back against the sofa cushion and propped her feet on the table in front of her. Duke really wanted her to ditch the story, and this time it was for her benefit, not his.

"A different path away from Timberline and this case?"

"My producer, Scott, isn't all that excited about this case anyway. I could dump it and he wouldn't blink an eye. In fact, he'd be happy since he tried to talk me out of the case to begin with. If I dropped the show, it would make him look good in his father's eyes, since his dad owns the production company."

"Seems we all want you to drop the story, don't we?"

He drained his cup of cider. "That was good. Do you want another or do you want to get something to eat?"

"I'm with Sue and Walt on this one. Maybe we can just order in. Pizza? Chinese?"

"Let's ask Gregory what he recommends."

Duke held out his hand and pulled her up from the sofa. She didn't want to let go, but he dropped her hand and put their empty cider cups on the tray.

"Gregory, my man. We're going to order in for dinner. Any recommendations?"

"There's a good pizza place down the road. They have pastas and salads, too." He pointed to the right of the reception desk. "There are a couple of menus there."

Beth reached for a red, white and green menu and held it up. "Vincenzo's?"

"That's it."

Duke joined her and hovered over her shoulder to look at the menu. "How come there's no restaurant on the premises?"

"I'm pretty sure Mr. Young made a deal with some of the town's restaurateurs to build the hotel only and not cut into their business."

"Jordan Young?" Beth ran her finger across the extra pizza ingredients.

"Yep. He developed the Timberline Hotel years ago. Bought the old one and renovated and expanded."

"He should update the security and get cameras in the hallways." Duke tapped the menu. "Pizza and salad?"

"That'll work." Beth shoved the menu into his hands. "You pick the pizza toppings and I'll grab a couple of twist-top bottles of wine."

"I have a better idea. I'll get the food and make a stop at a liquor store and pick up a decent bottle of cabernet."

"Sounds perfect. Do you want me to come with you?"

"I can handle it."

Beth tried to give him some cash, which he refused, and then went up to her room—the one right next to Duke's.

Not that she expected to get lucky tonight with that gorgeous man. She had a few things to tell him before they could reach that same level of intimacy they'd had before, which Beth had discovered hadn't been very deep.

Sleeping with a man didn't guarantee instant intimacy. She'd never had that level of intimacy with anyone before, but she'd come close with Duke. So close, the feeling had terrified her and she'd taken the surest route to torpedo the relationship.

She'd lied to Duke, betrayed him. He'd reacted as she'd expected him to—he dumped her. If she wanted him back, there could be no secrets between them.

Maybe tonight was the night—pizza, red wine and confidences.

When Beth returned to the room, she stepped into the shower and put on a pair of soft, worn jeans and the FBI Academy T-shirt Duke had given her two years ago. The shirt gave her confidence.

As soon as she turned on the TV, Duke knocked on the door. "Pizza man."

She peered through the peephole and opened the door. "I hope you got some paper plates and napkins."

"They're in the bag with the salad." He held up a bottle of wine. "Washington vineyard."

"This will be my third alcoholic beverage of the day. Really, this is unusual for me."

He placed the food on the credenza and turned to face her, his hands on his hips. "You don't have to excuse yourself just because my father was an alcoholic, Beth. Hell, you know I drink, too. I don't think a few drinks make you an alcoholic."

"I know that." She pulled the plates and napkins from the bag. "I just don't want you to get the wrong idea about me."

"I think I did have the wrong idea about you."

"I know." She popped open the plastic lid on the salad. "You thought you could trust me and I betrayed that trust."

"That's not it." He held up a corkscrew. "Bought a cheap one at the liquor store."

"What's not it?" She folded her arms across her stomach. Had he discovered something else about her?

"I've had plenty of time to think about what happened between us, and seeing you again and hearing your story has only confirmed what I'd begun to think about that time, about our relationship."

"Maybe I need some wine to hear this." Duke had uncorked the bottle, and Beth poured some of it into a plastic cup Duke had snagged from the cider setup in the lobby.

"It's nothing bad. I just didn't understand at the time that you took those files on purpose to push me away because we'd gotten too close, too fast."

The wine went down her throat the wrong way and

she choked. She covered her face with a napkin. "Have you now added psychology to your other talents?"

"Tell me it's not true." He tugged at the napkin.

"It wasn't conscious at the time. I just really, really wanted those files."

"You could've asked me."

"You would've said no."

"Probably." He tore off a piece of pizza and dropped it onto a paper plate. "All this analysis is making me hungry."

She peeked at him over the rim of her plastic cup. "Is that your way of telling me you forgive me for that incredibly stupid act?"

"Hey, that incredibly stupid act did solve the case, didn't it?"

"Only because I didn't reveal that other piece of info to you that I got from my source."

"Are you trying to make yourself look bad?"

"I just want you to see me, warts and all...this time. I... If there is a this time."

Duke took a big bite of pizza instead of answering her and she let it drop.

He had a better handle on discussing this kind of stuff than most men she knew because he'd been through court-mandated therapy as a teen when his father had beaten his mother to death after he'd accidentally killed his younger sister.

Such tragedy and he'd risen from the ashes a strong man, a good man—and she could've had him if she'd been able to recover from her own tragedies.

They watched TV together, she from the edge of the bed and he from a chair he'd pulled up, and ate their salad and pizza. A meal had never tasted better, but she stopped at two cups of wine. She needed the relaxation but also needed a clear head for her confession.

Duke collected her plate and cup and stuffed them into the white plastic bag. "More wine?"

"No, thanks. Save it. I may need it after my session with Scarlett tomorrow."

"Tomorrow?" He checked his phone. "You set it up for tomorrow?"

"Expecting a text?"

"Work." He tossed the phone on the bed. "What time are you seeing Scarlett and when did you arrange this?"

"When you'd gone outside her place to look around. I'm bringing my locket and heading out there at dusk."

"At night? Really?"

"She works during the day and needs the natural light. She suggested it. At least it's not the witching hour."

"I don't think you'd better call Scarlett a witch. She'd go off on you for sure."

"I wasn't calling her a witch." She pointed to the pizza box. "Breakfast tomorrow morning?"

"Works for me."

Beth licked a crumb from the corner of her mouth. Now, if only they could settle the sleeping arrangements for tonight as easily as that. She could always make a suggestion, but she didn't want to push things.

Duke swiped his thumb across his phone again and placed it on the credenza. "I'll take the trash outside. You don't want to be smelling garlic all night."

He grabbed the white bag and left the room.

Beth blew out a breath. He didn't say "*we* don't want

to be smelling garlic all night," so maybe he planned to go back to his own room.

She brushed some crumbs from the credenza into her palm just as Duke's phone vibrated. Was this the text he was expecting?

She spun the phone around to face her, touching the screen in the process. The phone was still unlocked from Duke's last usage.

The text message, from Mick Tedesco, sprang to life, and one word jumped out at Beth—*Brice*. Her eyes darted to the door and back to the phone.

She read the message aloud. "'The request to the Brices was sent and approved.'"

Pressing one hand to her heart, she stepped back. What request? Duke hadn't mentioned any request he'd made from the Brices. Did he plan to steal her thunder?

She heard the key at the door and retreated to the bathroom. How could she even ask him about it now without admitting she'd read his private text?

He stepped into the room. "That's better."

She poked her head out of the bathroom. "Would you mind taking the leftover pizza to your room when you leave?"

His step faltered for a second but he recovered quickly. "Sure. You want me to leave the wine here?"

"You can leave the wine." She ducked back into the bathroom and called out, "Don't forget your phone."

"Got it."

A few minutes later he stood at the bathroom door, his boots back on and holding the pizza box in front of him with the cell phone on top.

Holding her breath, her gaze darted to the phone.

Had he checked his very important message about the Brices yet?

"I'll see you tomorrow, Beth. And don't even think about going to Scarlett's without me."

"Of course not." She smiled as she unwound about a foot of dental floss. "We're partners in crime, right?"

A small vertical line formed between his eyebrows. "Right. Good night."

"Good night. Thanks for the pizza and wine."

When the door closed behind him, she threw the second bolt into place and marched to the credenza. She uncorked the wine and poured herself another generous glass.

Then she sat cross-legged on the bed and took a big gulp. It was a good thing she hadn't revealed her final secret to Duke…because the man was keeping one of his own.

Chapter Ten

Duke dropped the pizza box in his room and unlocked his phone to read Mick's message. Releasing a breath, he stretched out on the bed and texted him back. Rush order?

A few minutes later Mick confirmed and Duke ate another piece of pizza to celebrate. He'd hoped to celebrate another way tonight, but Beth had made it clear that she'd expected him to spend the night in his own room. Maybe she hadn't bought his forgiveness-and-understanding shtick, even though he'd been dead serious.

He didn't blame her for not trusting him. As recently as two days ago he'd been railing against her for her actions two years ago. That was before he'd discovered her real purpose for being in Timberline.

He finished the pizza and got up to brush his teeth. He leaned forward and studied his face in the mirror.

Maybe Beth had it right. This time they should take things slow and easy and not jump to any conclusions about each other.

He could do that.

Could she?

Duke spent the next day in meetings with the local FBI office and on the phone with the Drug Enforcement Agency. He'd touched base with Beth a few times and she'd been busy conducting more interviews and visiting relevant sites like the house of Kayla Rush's kidnapping.

He just wanted to make sure she didn't go out to Scarlett Easton's house by herself. He didn't trust those hunters—or anyone else in this town.

He ended his day in the sheriff's station, shooting the breeze with Unger. Musgrove had gone golfing with the mayor and Jordan Young.

"The local hunters don't much care for Scarlett Easton?"

"She complains about them a lot. She just doesn't like hunting."

"They've done things like that before? Shoot close to her property?"

"Sure, but they've never come close to hitting someone, like they did with Ms. St. Regis."

"Yeah." Duke chewed the edge of his fingernail. "Do you think it was on purpose?"

"I'm not sure. Maybe someone was trying to scare her off, like with the broken window and the frog head, but that's extreme."

"If the guy was a good shot, he wouldn't see it as extreme since he never intended for the bullet to hit its mark."

"Still, that could be attempted murder."

"You and I know that, but someone willing to take that chance in the first place—" Unger shrugged "—that might not occur to him."

"I told Beth I'd ask you about your mom, if she'd be willing to talk to her about the Brices and what happened twenty-five years ago."

"I'd hate for my mom to wind up on TV."

"I understand. What if I could guarantee that her interview wouldn't leave Beth's possession?"

"Then why would Beth want to interview my mother if she didn't plan to use it for the segment?"

Toying with the edge of a folder, Duke said, "Information."

"Is that why Beth was talking to Scarlett Easton? Information? Because I can't imagine Scarlett wanting to get involved with a TV show. I don't think she even watches TV."

"Just a different perspective. These shows collect all kinds of footage and info they never use."

Unger lifted his shoulders. "I'll see what I can do."

"Thanks, man." Duke checked his phone. Did five o'clock qualify as dusk? "I'm outta here. Keep me posted on any new developments in the Gary Binder hit and run."

"Will do."

When Duke pulled into the parking lot of the Timberline Hotel, his shoulders relaxed when he spotted Beth's rental car. He'd had a nagging feeling all day that she'd take off without him.

He waved to Gregory at the front desk, avoided Walt and Sue in the lobby and jogged up the two flights of stairs to Beth's room. As he knocked on the door, he called, "Beth, it's Duke."

She opened the door. "I saw Scarlett in town. We're meeting at seven."

"Do you want to get something to eat on the way?"

"I had a bite to eat in town. I'll knock when I'm ready to go. About thirty minutes?"

"I'll be ready."

She shut the door in his face.

Had she read his mind and his body language last night? He'd wanted to bed her and, up until last night, he'd thought she'd wanted the same thing.

Maybe he wouldn't get a second chance with Beth, but he still planned to make sure nothing happened to her on this wild-goose chase.

He'd had a big lunch with the FBI boys and figured he could skip dinner, anyway. He showered instead and changed out of his suit. He didn't know what to wear to a haunting, but he was pretty sure it wasn't a suit.

At around six forty-five, Beth tapped on his door.

He greeted her by jingling his car keys. "Let's take my SUV. It has four-wheel drive. Her place is remote, even by Timberline standards."

"Okay." She nervously toyed with a chain around her neck.

"Is that the locket?"

"This is it." She held it out from her neck with her thumb, where a gold heart dangled from the delicate chain.

As they hit the stairwell, Duke said, "I've worked with psychics a few times on cases. While they haven't solved anything for us, there's definitely something there."

"I hope Scarlett can tell me something. Even if it's some small connection to the Brices, it might be enough."

"Enough for what?" Duke pushed open the door to the lobby.

"Enough to warrant some communication with them,

but like I said before, I don't want to give them any false hope."

"False hope is never good, especially in cases like this."

She tilted her head and shot him a quizzical look from beneath her lashes before she got into the car.

He started the car. "I'm guessing you didn't get to interview Jordan Young today."

"I didn't. How'd you know that?"

"I dropped by the sheriff's station to see Cody— Deputy Unger—and he told me Sheriff Musgrove was out playing golf with Young and the mayor." He snapped his fingers. "Mayor Burton. Have you met him yet?"

"Not yet. I spent my day videotaping different locations…and replacing my frog."

"You bought another?"

"I wanted to ask Linda, the shop owner, if anyone had come into the store after me or had asked about me later."

"Any luck?"

"Nothing suspicious, anyway. A few people chatted with her about the show, but these were people she knew. She was happy to sell me another frog, though."

"Are you going to keep this one under lock and key?" Duke made the turn off the main highway and the sky immediately darkened as the trees grew thicker.

"I'm going to guard him with my life."

He glanced sideways at her, expecting a smile, but Beth's jaw had a hard line that worried the hell out of him. How long had she been obsessed by this? He'd never seen this side to her two years ago.

As much time as they'd spent together, as many times as they'd made love, he'd never really known her.

The SUV bounced over the rough road and Beth clutched the locket against her throat.

"Are you having second thoughts? Because we can turn right around."

"No. Scarlett said it would be tougher on her than me."

"It's probably not going to be any picnic for you, either, especially if you discover something you weren't expecting."

"I have to do this."

"I know you do." He squeezed her thigh beneath the soft denim of her jeans. "And I'm gonna be right there with you."

She gave him a stiff nod.

He parked the car at the edge of the stand of trees circling Scarlett's house. He poked Beth in the arm. "Any more bullets start flying, hit the ground—and I'm only half kidding."

"Do you see me laughing?"

He kept an arm around Beth's shoulders as they approached the house, even though she'd stiffened beneath his touch. This meeting with Scarlett had put her on edge and he feared she'd drop over into the abyss.

As THEY REACHED the porch, Beth shrugged off Duke's arm. She didn't need a protector, especially one who kept important secrets from her. When was he going to tell her what he was doing with the Brices? Had he actually told them about her quest?

The heavy knocker that sported a bear's head gleamed

under the porch light. Duke lifted it and tapped it against the plate several times.

Scarlett answered the door in a pair of black yoga pants and an oversize sweater that hung almost to her knees. "Did you bring the locket?"

"Right here." Beth held it out from her neck.

"Come in and have a seat by the fire." Her gaze raked Duke up and down. "Did that worthless sheriff tell you anything about the shot fired on my property yesterday?"

"He had a couple of deputies searching for a shell casing this morning, but that's about as efficient as searching for a needle in a haystack, and he sent a notice out to the hunters."

She tossed her long braid over one shoulder. "That figures. Do you want something to drink before we get started?"

"You girls aren't going to start tossing back whiskeys again, are you?" Duke raised one eyebrow and his mouth quirked into a smile as Scarlett gave a low chuckle.

Beth's gaze darted between Duke and Scarlett and something tightened in her chest. He liked her. What wasn't to like? The woman was gorgeous with her long, dark hair, mocha skin and sumptuous figure. Even the baggy sweater seemed to hug her curves.

The artist had an earth-mother figure, a body made for childbearing. Beth ran her hands down her own slim hips and a sob caught in her throat.

"I'm drinking a special tea tonight." Scarlett put her hand on Beth's arm. "Can I get you a cup? You look pale."

"That would be nice, thanks."

"You—" Scarlett leveled a finger at Duke "—don't

look like a hot-tea kind of guy. Would you like a shot of that whiskey?"

"I don't touch the hard stuff, but I could use a beer."

Scarlett called over her shoulder as she sauntered into the kitchen. "You might need another when this is all over."

Beth sat in a chair near the huge natural-stone fireplace and curled out her fingers to the flame. "Is this okay here?"

"I'm going to sit in front of the fireplace on the floor." She must've already brewed the tea because she came out of the kitchen carrying two steaming cups. "Do you want sugar or milk?"

"No, thanks." She took the mug from Scarlett and sniffed the slightly bitter aroma of the pale brown tea.

Scarlett put her own cup on the broad base of the fireplace and returned to the kitchen for Duke's beer. Then she settled on a rug in front of the fire and took a sip of tea.

"A… Are there some times that are better for you to do this than others?"

"Like a full moon or something?" Scarlett shrugged. "No. You have the gift or you don't."

Beth sucked some tea onto her tongue and wrinkled her nose. Maybe she should've gone with the sugar.

Scarlett studied her over the rim of her mug. "Doesn't taste very good, does it? It's an acquired taste. I make it myself from roots and berries—an old recipe handed down through the generations."

With trembling fingers, Beth reached for the clasp on her locket. "I suppose you want this."

Three tries and she still couldn't unlatch the necklace.

"Let me." Duke crouched beside her and brushed her hair from the back of her neck. His warm fingers against her nape caused a thrill of excitement to race through her body despite the occasion. His touch always caused an immediate reaction in her body.

"Got it." He held out his hand where the chain pooled in his palm. He leaned forward and dumped the necklace into Scarlett's outstretched hand.

"May I?" She paused, her thumbnail against the crease of the locket.

Beth nodded and Scarlett popped open the gold heart. She flattened it open between two fingers. "This could be your hair—this strawberry blond. The blond could even be your hair at another age."

"That'll help, though, won't it? To have some hair as well as the locket?"

"It might." Scarlett crossed her legs beneath her and stretched her arms toward the fire, her dark eyes glittering in the firelight. "There are a few rules we need to cover."

"Rules?" Beth glanced at Duke.

"No matter what happens, do not bring me out of my trance."

"You're going into a trance?"

"What did you expect?" Scarlett's dark eyebrows jumped to her hairline. "Did you think I was going to search for your locket on the internet?"

"But a trance? Is it dangerous?" Beth bit her lip.

"Draining, but not dangerous—unless you yank me out of it." Scarlett tugged on her braid. "No matter what happens, no matter what I say or do, even if it looks like I'm having some kind of seizure."

"Seizure? Oh, my God. I can't let you do this, Scarlett."

"I've already decided I'm doing it. Like I said, I have my own reasons."

Duke sat on the floor next to Beth's chair and curved his hand around her calf. "Let her continue, Beth. Scarlett knows what she's doing."

"Listen to your man." Scarlett closed her eyes and cradled her mug. She took a long sip and placed it on the stone of the fireplace.

Her eyes opened to slits and she slipped her finger beneath the chain of the necklace and dangled it in front of the fire. The golden locket seemed infused with a flame as it swung from Scarlett's finger.

She curled her hand around the locket and held it in her fist. She exhaled slowly and her lids fell over her eyes.

Scarlett whispered something under her breath, but Beth didn't catch it. She raised her brows at Duke and he shook his head.

The whispers became a silent movement of the lips as Scarlett's knuckles turned white. Her head lolled back, her long braid almost touching the rug beneath her.

Scarlett's eyelids began flickering and her lips twitched.

Beth slid to the floor beside Duke, tucking her hand in the crook of his arm. She touched his ear with her lips. "I hope she's okay."

"I hope so, too."

Scarlett's chin dipped to her chest, her body still.

Beth whispered, "Did she fall asleep? Is this the trance she was talking about?"

Duke curled his arm around her waist and pulled her

closer. "Shh. I don't know, Beth. I've never seen anything like this before."

Beth watched Scarlett's still form and it seemed as if the fire was swirling around her. Scarlett's long hair became the flames, dancing and curling around her face.

Beth put two fingers to her throbbing temple.

Duke whispered, "What's wrong?"

"I feel strange." She looked at the dregs floating in her cup. "Do you think that tea was some kind of drug?"

"What do you mean, like peyote or mushrooms?"

"I don't know." Beth ran her tongue along her dry teeth. "I feel funny."

"It is hot in here."

Scarlett gave a sharp cry and her head jerked back. Her lids flew open but her eyes had rolled back in her head.

"Duke!" Beth grabbed his hand. "Do something."

"You heard what she told us. We could actually do more harm than good if we interrupt her."

Scarlett brought one hand to her throat, clutching at it and gasping for breath.

Beth dug her nails into Duke's hand. She couldn't let this go on. What if something happened to Scarlett in this altered state?

Duke's arm tightened around her, as if he could read her thoughts. "Wait."

Scarlett gave another strangled cry and the hand not clutching the locket shot out. She grabbed Beth's upper arm, her grip like a vise. She pulled Beth toward her, toward the fire in the grate.

Duke held on to her, making her a rope in a tug-of-war.

"Let me go, Duke."

He released his hold on her and she allowed Scarlett to drag her beside her on the rug. Scarlett's hand slipped to Beth's and she laced her fingers with hers.

A flash jolted Beth's body. She could hear Duke's voice calling to her a million miles away as she traveled through darkness scattered with pinpoints of light. The heat from the fire had disappeared and a bone-chilling cold gripped her body. The blackness turned to a deep forest green, rushing and rustling past her.

Then it stopped. She jerked to a halt. The rushing sound became voices—loud, yelling, screaming, crying.

She smelled it before she saw it—metallic, pungent—blood. So much blood, waves of it, slick, wet. A baby crying.

Beth gagged, ripping her hand from Scarlett's.

Scarlett dropped the locket and pressed her palms against either side of her head. "The blood. The blood. So much blood."

Duke lunged forward and hooked his hands beneath Beth's arms, hoisting her up and against his chest. "Are you all right? What the hell was that?"

Beth's eyes felt so heavy she could barely raise them to Duke's face. "Blood."

"Sit." He pushed her into the chair and then hunched over Scarlett. "Are you okay, Scarlett? Should I get you anything?"

"Water, bring us some water." She stretched out on her back, flinging one arm across her eyes.

A few minutes later Duke pressed a glass to Beth's lips. "Drink."

She gulped the water so fast it dribbled down her

chin and she didn't even care. After she downed the glass, she looked up, blinking, clearing her vision.

Scarlett's eyes met hers. "You saw it, too, didn't you?"

Beth nodded.

Dragging his hands through his dark hair, Duke paced to the window and back. "What the hell just happened? Did you drag Beth into your vision? Did you drug her?"

"Hold on there, cowboy." Scarlett held up her index finger. "That tea is not a drug. Yes, it does enhance my visions, but I had no idea it would have any effect on Beth. That's never happened before."

"What's never happened before? You giving someone that witch's brew or you dragging someone into your trance?"

Scarlett pressed her lips into a thin line and then she flicked her fingers at Duke. "How are you feeling, Beth?"

"I feel fine, amazing actually. It was like an out-of-body experience."

"Can you please get Beth more water instead of blustering around the room?"

Duke's mouth opened, shut, and then he growled. He took Beth's glass and stormed off to the kitchen.

"You'll be fine, Beth. I'm sorry I grabbed your hand like that. I am telling the truth. I've never done that before, didn't even know it was a possibility."

"Never mind all that. What did we see?"

"You tell me. What did *you* see?"

Beth's lashes fluttered. "I saw... I smelled blood. I

heard people yelling and screaming. I heard a child or a baby crying."

"Amazing." Scarlett shook her head. "That's what I got, too. You shared my vision."

"What does it mean, Scarlett?" Beth took the glass from Duke and gave him a small smile. It didn't seem like he liked Scarlett all that much anymore.

"What do you think it means?" Scarlett settled her back against the base of the fireplace.

"If it's connected to the locket I had before my adoption, it has something to do with my past. Could it be the scene of my kidnapping?"

"Whoa, wait a minute." Duke held out one hand. "There was no mention of blood at your kidnapping. There was no blood spilled at any of the kidnappings."

Beth tapped her water glass with one fingernail. "Could it just be a representation of the violence of my kidnapping, Scarlett?"

"I'm not sure about that. I guess so." She stood up and stretched. "Did you recognize the place?"

"The place?"

"The cabin. I'm pretty sure it was a cabin."

"Oh." Beth slumped back in the chair. "I didn't see a place, just the blood, the smells, the sounds."

"That's another problem. Heather Brice was kidnapped from her parents' house, which was not a cabin." Duke jerked his thumb at the necklace still glinting on the rug where Scarlett had dropped it. "How do you know this... vision has anything to do with you? It could be something connected to the previous owner of the locket. Right, Scarlett?"

"I suppose so, but I was compelled to take Beth's hand, to bring her in."

"The facts are you don't have a clue what you're doing here. You drink some herbal tea, you utter some mumbo jumbo, you have some visions and you leave your clients with more questions than answers."

"Clients?" Scarlett widened her stance and tossed her braid over her shoulder. "I'm an artist. The only clients I have are the ones who buy my art and sponsor my shows."

"Duke, Scarlett agreed to do this because I asked her. While frightened by what I saw and heard, I'm satisfied with what we did here tonight."

"Okay." Duke clasped the back of his neck and tipped his head from side to side. "I'm sorry, Scarlett. I just don't see how this helps Beth."

Beth bent down to sweep up her necklace. "What else did you see, Scarlett? Anything more about the cabin? I didn't join your vision until later. You must've experienced more than I did."

"It was a cabin, a nice one, and it had a red door. I can't tell you anything else specific about it—I didn't see the location, any particular furnishings or the people in it."

Duke snorted and Beth shot him a warning glance.

"But I did see two birds."

"Flying around? That's helpful."

Beth jabbed Duke in the ribs for his sarcastic tone, but Scarlett didn't seem to notice.

"There were two birds…over the fireplace? I'm not sure. I just remember two birds—maybe on a painting, maybe they were those hideous stuffed taxidermy things."

"Anything else?"

"The people—there was a man, a woman and a child, wasn't there?"

"I certainly heard voices, but I'm not sure I could distinguish them, and I did hear a baby or a child crying."

"And the hair." Scarlett reached out and lifted a strand of Beth's hair. "The woman had strawberry blond hair."

Chapter Eleven

Beth took another turn around the hotel room. "What do you think it means? A woman with strawberry blond hair?"

"Who knows? Scarlett Easton is not exactly an expert at interpretation, is she?"

"She never claimed to be." Beth wedged her hands on her hips. "Why did you start attacking Scarlett when she was just trying to help me?"

"Help you? By dragging you into her dream state? I thought—" He raked a hand through his hair. "I was worried about you."

Beth gave him a sidelong glance. "I thought you had a thing for her."

"Scarlett's not my type—too artsy, too reclusive, too...weird." Folding his arms, he leaned against the window. "Would you care if I did have a thing for Scarlett?"

Before he'd started keeping secrets from her? Hell, yeah. Now?

She splayed her hands in front of her. "She's a beautiful woman. I could understand the attraction."

Rolling his shoulders, he pushed off the window. "What

are you going to do with the information? What does it prove?"

Duke wasn't going to take the bait.

"It proves—" she dropped to the bed "—that I was in a cabin here as a child, before the Kings adopted me. I plan to locate that cabin."

"And you're going to do that how? By running around Timberline and looking into all the cabins with red doors?"

"It's a start."

"Then what?"

She fell back on the bed and stared at the ceiling. "Why are you trying to discourage me? I thought you were all in. I thought you were going to help me with this."

"That was before someone hit and killed Gary Binder, before someone started taking shots at you in the forest."

"Gary's death doesn't have anything to do with me, and that shot could've been a hunter harassing Scarlett."

"You're doing it again, Beth." The mattress sank as Duke sat on the edge of the bed. "You're so single-mindedly focused on one goal you're not seeing the whole picture."

"I don't care about the whole picture." She puffed out a breath and a strand of hair floated above her face and settled against her lips. "I need to do this. Scarlett has given me the first real lead since I got here and I'm going to follow up on it."

He shifted on the bed and she held her breath. If he took her in his arms right now and kissed her, she'd kiss him back and to hell with the secrets between them— his and hers.

Standing above her, he shook his head. "Stubborn woman. I'll help you."

Bracing her elbows against the bed, she hoisted herself up. "I'll do it with or without you, but thanks."

"Get some sleep." He nudged her foot and stalked to the door, mumbling as if to himself. "What else am I going to do, let you wander around the woods on your own like Little Red Riding Hood?"

The door slammed behind him and Beth narrowed her eyes.

He could start by telling her the truth about what he was doing with the Brices.

BETH USED HER interviews the next day to discreetly ask about cabins in the area. She also scanned her videos to see if any of the cabins she'd captured had red doors— they didn't.

After her third interview of the morning, Beth slumped behind the wheel of her rental and gave Jordan Young's office another call. His assistant answered after the first ring.

"This is Beth St. Regis again. Just checking to see if Mr. Young has some time today for that interview."

"I'm sorry, Ms. St. Regis. Mr. Young is out of town today, but I know he's looking forward to talking to you."

"I know he's busy. Just tell him I called again and I'm available at his convenience."

"Will do."

Beth's stomach growled and she patted it. She'd skipped out on breakfast this morning because she hadn't wanted to share an awkward meal with Duke. The other night he must've thought they were growing closer, putting their bitter past behind them. He'd even apologized for cutting her off, had admitted misunderstanding her.

She could've had it all back with him if she hadn't seen that text from his boss, Mickey Tedesco. She could ask him about it point-blank, get it out in the open. Of course, then she'd have to admit she'd been sneaking around again and delving into his business.

Was that wrong if he really was keeping secrets from her? It was like the cheating spouse. If your spouse was stepping out on you, didn't that sort of excuse your checking his emails and text messages?

She exited her car and turned up her collar against the wind. A drop of rain spattered against the back of her hand and she hunched forward and made a beeline for the sandwich shop on the corner.

Ducking inside, she brushed droplets of moisture from her hair. The shop was more of a take-out place, but it did boast several wrought-iron tables to one side.

She ordered an Italian sub at the counter, picked out a bag of chips and waited for the self-serve soft-drink machine. The guy at the machine turned suddenly and almost spilled his drink on her.

"Sorry… Ms. St. Regis."

"Deputy Unger, how are you?" Her gaze dipped to his flannel shirt and jeans. "Off duty?"

"Yes." He held up a plastic bag, bulging with food. "Just picking up some lunch for my hunting trip."

"Oh, you hunt, too." She wrinkled her nose. She was with Scarlett on her distaste of the so-called sport.

"Most of us grow up hunting in these parts…and I always eat my game. I go for the turkey—" he pointed at the take-out counter "—probably a lot like your sandwich."

"I admit it. I'm a city girl. I don't understand the sport."

He sealed a plastic lid on his cup and grabbed a straw. "I talked to my mom about your show. She's actually okay with it."

Beth's heart did a somersault in her chest. "That would be great. Thanks so much for talking to her."

Unger pounded his straw against the counter. "I think she would've contacted you on her own. She heard you were in town doing the story."

"I'm sure a few words from her son didn't hurt." And a few words from Duke to Unger on her behalf.

Unger grabbed a napkin and asked the guy behind the counter for a pen. "Here's her number. Feel free to call her anytime. She's a retired schoolteacher and spends her days with knitting groups and book clubs and volunteering at the public library, but I think this is one of her free days if you have an opening."

"I do." She folded the napkin and tucked it in her purse. "I've been trying to set up something with Jordan Young, but he's never available."

"Yeah, Jordan. He's a big wheeler-dealer in town—has been for years. He seems to get the sweetest deals. We all joke that he must have a dossier on every public official."

"Sounds like he knows the town's secrets."

"He's been here for a long time, even though he's not a local. Came out of nowhere, married a local girl and set up shop pretty quickly—successful guy."

"Which is why he's hard to pin down." She patted

her purse where she'd stashed his mother's phone number. "Thanks again."

"Save your thanks until after the interview. My mom just might talk your ear off." Taking a sip from his soda, he held up his hand and left the shop.

She filled her cup with ice and root beer and picked up her sandwich from the counter. She'd have to thank Duke for this interview.

As she sat down, Jason Foster walked through the door. He approached her table. "Hey, Beth. How'd it go with my cousin?"

"We, uh, talked."

"She's a trip, huh?"

Trip—yeah, that was exactly the word she'd use.

"I like her."

"Some do, some don't. Did she tell you anything?" He waved to the guy at the counter. "You got my pastrami?"

"She was helpful."

"Dang, that's not a word I'd use for my cuz." He pointed at the counter. "I have to pick up my lunch and get back to work. Glad Scarlett could help."

He paid for his sandwich and left the store.

She didn't know how close Scarlett and Jason were, but she didn't feel comfortable talking about what went on at Scarlett's cabin. Hell, she didn't even know what had happened there.

She finished her lunch with no more interruptions and then pulled out the napkin with Mrs. Unger's telephone number.

Her anticipation was dashed when she heard the

woman's voice mail. Beth left a message and got up to refill her soda.

Her phone started ringing and Beth sprinted back to the table and grabbed it. "Hello?"

"Is this Beth St. Regis from the *Cold Case Chronicles* show?"

"Yes. Mrs. Unger?"

"You can call me Dorothy."

"Dorothy, thanks for calling back." Beth pulled out her chair and sat down. "Your son said you'd be willing to talk to me about the Timberline Trio case, specifically about the Brices, since you knew them well."

"Such a sad time." Dorothy clicked her tongue. "I'd be happy to talk to you, Beth. Do you think I'll be on TV?"

Beth's lips twisted into a smile. "I'm not sure. It just depends. From what your son said, I thought you wouldn't be interested."

"Oh, that's Cody talking. Who wouldn't want to be on TV?"

"Can we meet at your house or wherever you're comfortable?"

"You can come by now if you like. I have a knitting circle at three o'clock, but I'm free until then."

"Perfect."

Dorothy gave Beth her address and she punched it into her phone's GPS.

A half an hour later, Beth reached Dorothy's house, which was located in one of the newer tracks and easy to find.

She pulled into the driveway behind an old but immaculate compact and retrieved her video camera and tripod from the trunk of her rental.

Before she walked up to the front door, she sent a quick text to Duke thanking him for convincing Unger to let her have access to his mother—even if Dorothy would've contacted her on her own.

Hitching the camera case over her shoulder, she walked up the two steps of the porch and rang the doorbell.

A small, neat woman who mirrored the small, neat compact in the driveway answered the door. "Hello, Beth."

"Dorothy. Thanks for talking with me."

"Of course. Come in. Coffee? Water?" She winked. "Something a little stronger?"

What was it with the Washington women and their whiskey? Must be the cold, damp weather.

"No, thank you. I just had lunch."

"Do you need to set up that camera?"

"I do." Beth gestured to the sofa where a magazine had been placed facedown on one of the cushions. "Sit where you're comfortable."

Dorothy sat on the sofa and folded her hands in her lap. "Is this a good place for lighting and all that?"

Beth extended her tripod on the other side of the coffee table in front of the sofa. "I'm no cameraperson. I have someone who does that for me. I'm just here doing some preliminary interviews. Just casual."

"Oh, thank goodness. Then I have nothing to be nervous about."

"Of course not." Beth's fingers trembled as she touched the video camera's display for the settings. She was the nervous one. This woman could've actually known her as a toddler.

Beth started the interview in the usual manner. Dorothy stated her name, address and the current date, and Beth questioned her about what she remembered twenty-five years ago.

It didn't differ much from the other accounts. The suspicions about Kayla Rush's father, and then the shock of Stevie Carson's disappearance, and the sheer terror when the toddler Heather Brice went missing.

"Three children snatched—" Dorothy snapped her fingers "—just like that. Those of us with young kids were terrified. I didn't let my boys out of my sight for one second for months after the kidnappings."

"And you were close with the Brices at the time?"

"We were friendly, socialized. Timberline wasn't as populated in those days. Evergreen Software brought in a lot of new people."

"Do you remember Heather?"

"A sweet little girl."

"She had blond hair, didn't she?" Beth had been twisting her own hair around one finger and dropped it. "I saw some fuzzy newspaper photos of her."

"It was blond, just like her mother's, although Patty had a little help from her hairdresser."

"Blond?" A knot formed in Beth's gut. "Mrs. Brice was a blonde?"

"She had been. Like I said, she lightened her hair. I think her real color was light brown."

Beth fingered the necklace around her neck. Light brown, not strawberry blond? She dropped the locket against her chest. That didn't mean anything. The woman in Scarlett's vision could've been the kidnapper.

"Was there some evidence regarding hair?"

"No, no. I was just thinking about some pictures I saw that were related to the case."

Beth asked more questions about the family, as many as she could without arousing Dorothy's suspicions again.

She ended the interview with a warm feeling in her belly. By all accounts, the Brices were a close and loving family. They would welcome their long-lost daughter with open arms.

As Beth shut off the camera, she asked, "Did Mr. Brice already have his money when he lived here?"

"They were wealthy because Charlie had sold his first patent, but nothing compared to what they are now." Dorothy dragged the magazine into her lap and smoothed her hands over the glossy cover. "If little Heather had been kidnapped first, everyone would've expected a ransom note."

"Did you keep in touch with the family when they left town?"

"Exchanged a few Christmas cards, but I think Patty and Charlie wanted to put this chapter behind them."

"With all their money, did they ever do a private search for Heather?"

"I'm sure they did, but she never told me about it. They moved two years later." Dorothy pushed out of the sofa. "Would you like something now?"

"Water would be great."

Dorothy called from the kitchen. "I think I have a few pictures of Heather with my boys, if you're interested, but I'd have to find them."

Beth's heart thumped in her chest. She'd seen only the old newspaper pictures of Heather Brice. She'd felt no sense of recognition, but that didn't mean anything. Maybe clearer, color photos would reveal more.

"I'd love to see them if you can find them."

Dorothy returned with a glass of water. "I'll look later and give you a call if I have anything useful."

Beth took a few sips of water. "Do you know of any cabins around here that have red doors?"

"Not now, not anymore."

Beth's hand froze, the glass halfway to her lips. "Not anymore? There was one before?"

"There were several. It was a trend."

"How long ago was this, Dorothy?" Beth wiped her mouth with the back of her hand.

"Maybe thirty, thirty-five years ago. Designs follow trends, don't they? Remember the hideous avocado-green appliances? Now everything has to be stainless steel."

"How many cabins had these red doors?"

"Ten or fifteen?" She peered at Beth. "Why? Is this some new evidence, too?"

"I can't say right now. Were these cabins in the same area or scattered around?"

"I can't remember, Beth. They were here and there. Who knew at the time that any of this stuff would be important?"

"Are there any left? Any cabins with red doors?"

"There might be a few. You'd probably want to talk to a Realtor—not that lush Bill Raney, but you could try Rebecca Geist. She's a sharp gal. Just sold Cass Teagan's place."

"Maybe I will. I've seen a few of her open houses around."

"When are you going to make a decision about the story and the footage?"

"I'll submit everything to my producer and he'll make the decision. Then the rest of my crew will come out and we'll put a story together."

"You won't solve it and neither will that handsome young FBI agent who's out here now." Dorothy put her finger to her lips and said in a hushed voice, "I'm beginning to believe it really was that Quileute basket lady who steals children away and eats them."

BETH COLLAPSED IN her car, a range of emotions assaulting her brain. Whose strawberry blond hair was in her locket? Her own? If so, who was the strawberry blonde Scarlett had seen in the vision? Maybe Scarlett had seen her as an adult.

Her mind shifted, another scattered piece of information in her brain taking shape, like a figure in a kaleidoscope.

Was there a way to find all those cabins that had red doors? If she tracked down each one, would she discover the cabin from her trance?

She threw her car into Reverse and backed out of Dorothy's driveway. She needed to touch base with Scarlett again. Had the shaman remembered more from her dream state?

She drove across town and hit the main highway. She took the turnoff, watching for the colorful mailbox that marked Scarlett's private access road.

Duke hadn't wanted her to come out here by herself, but he'd been busy all day and this couldn't wait. She pulled up when she saw the mailbox and tapped Duke's number on her cell phone.

"Where are you? I've been texting you for the past thirty minutes." His voice was gruff.

"I didn't get your texts. I'm on my way to see Scarlett."

"Damn it, Beth. You couldn't wait for me?"

"It's broad daylight."

"It was broad daylight last time. Stay put. I'm on my way."

"I'm at Scarlett's mailbox at the beginning of the access road. I'll just drive up to her place and wait for you. I don't even know if she's home."

"Stay in your car."

"Duke, I think you're overreacting."

"Let me overreact if it keeps you safe."

She ended the call and swung onto the access road leading to Scarlett's cabin. The rough road bounced and jostled her car, and she drove it as far as the road allowed.

She grabbed the handle, cracked the door open and stopped. She'd promised Duke she'd wait in the car until he got there—a ridiculous precaution, but one she'd honor.

Tipping her head back against the headrest, Beth drummed out a rhythm against the steering wheel and then checked the time on her cell phone. Scarlett must not be home if she hadn't heard Beth's car drive up the road.

She swung the car door open the rest of the way and dragged in a deep lungful of the pine-scented air. The mist caressing the copse of trees ringing Scarlett's cabin gave the area a mythical, mystical quality that suited its inhabitant.

A loud wail shattered the peace, sending a river of chills down her spine. She jumped out of the car and hung on the car door. "Hello? Scarlett?"

An animalistic shriek pierced the air and Beth bolted from the car and ran down the small path that wound its way through the trees to Scarlett's cabin. The front porch came into view and Beth charged ahead.

A vise grabbed her ankle with a snap and Beth tumbled forward onto her hands and knees as a sharp pain knifed up her leg. She hit the ground with a cry and rolled to her back to take pressure off her ankle.

Her eyes watering, she glanced at her injured leg and choked. A trap had her in its steely grip.

Chapter Twelve

Duke cursed when he saw Beth's car and the open door. Why didn't it surprise him that she hadn't stayed put like he'd asked? When had Beth St. Regis ever played it safe?

He slammed his car door and stalked to her rental. The open door gave him pause. He poked his head inside the car and swallowed. Why'd she leave her keys in the ignition and phone in the cup holder?

A low moan floated through the trees and he jerked his head up, the blood pounding in his ears. "Beth?"

"Duke? Duke, I'm here. Help me."

He crashed through the trees, and when he saw Beth on the ground, crumpled in pain, he rushed to her side. He dropped next to her, reaching for the cruel trap that had her boot in its teeth.

"Oh, my God. Did the spikes reach your flesh?"

Her chin wobbled. "I can't tell. It's almost numb with pain. I'm afraid to move or I would've crawled to my car to get my phone."

"Where's Scarlett?" He twisted his head over his shoulder.

"I don't know. I haven't seen anyone since I arrived." She ended with a hiss.

"Stretch out your leg. I'm gonna get this thing off of you."

Slowly she extended her leg, the trap clamped onto her ankle.

Duke placed both hands on either side of the trap's jaws and pulled them apart. The spring jumped and the trap snapped open.

The teeth of the trap had mangled Scarlett's boot, but he didn't see any blood. "I don't see any blood, but I'm going to leave it to the medical professionals to remove your boot."

"Thank God I was wearing them. My foot and ankle hurt like hell, but it's just a mass of pain. I can't tell what's injured."

"Let's get you to the hospital." He scooped her up and tromped back the way he'd come, keeping his eyes on the ground for any more surprises.

"Somebody placed that trap there on purpose, Duke, and lured me out of my car."

"How?" His arms tightened around her and he could feel the erratic fluttering of her heart against his chest.

"I heard wailing and a scream. It sounded like a wounded animal, but it could've been human." She tugged on his jacket. "We need to warn Scarlett. There may be more traps set around her cabin."

"I'm calling the sheriff's department." He settled her into the passenger seat and placed a kiss on top of her head, where his lips met beads of dew clinging to the strands of her hair.

"And Scarlett. That trap could've just as well been meant for her."

"Or you." When he got behind the wheel, he pulled

his phone from his pocket. At Beth's urging, his first call went to Scarlett.

"Hello?"

"Scarlett, it's Duke Harper. I'm just leaving your place with Beth, who stepped into a trap outside your cabin."

Scarlett sucked in a sharp breath. "What kind of trap?"

"I'm not sure, but it could be a bear trap."

"A trap? You mean a real animal trap?"

"That's what it looks like to me."

"Is she okay?"

"I'm taking her to the hospital emergency room, but be careful. There might be more traps around your cabin."

"The police?"

"I'm calling the sheriff next. Where are you?"

"I'm at my granny's place on the reservation. How the hell did a bear trap get on my property?"

"I was hoping you could tell us."

"Duke, it could've been meant for me. It might not have anything to do with Beth."

"Yeah, except she's the one who was trapped."

He ended the call with Scarlett and tapped his phone for the sheriff's department. He told them about the wounded animal sound Beth had heard and gave them the location of the trap he'd removed from her ankle.

Tossing the phone onto the console, he said, "Scarlett thinks the trap could've been meant for her."

"It could've been meant for either one of us." Beth winced and rubbed her thigh.

"You doing okay? Hang in there." He sped back toward town, taking the bypass road to the new hospital near Evergreen Software.

He pulled up to the emergency room entrance and carried Beth inside. "She needs a wheelchair. She stepped onto a trap and injured her foot or ankle."

An orderly burst through the swinging doors, pushing a wheelchair.

Duke put her into the chair and followed the orderly back to the examination rooms.

The orderly lifted Beth onto an exam table and said, "A nurse will be right with you."

The paper on the exam table crinkled as Beth hoisted herself up onto her elbows. "Who would do that? You know that trap was deliberately set."

"Of course it was, but who was the prey? You or Scarlett?"

She crossed her arms over her chest like a shield. "It's Scarlett's place. No one could know for sure if I'd be back there, but Scarlett would be there, guaranteed."

"Just seems odd that both of these attacks at Scarlett's cabin happened when you were there. Is Scarlett even in an active battle with the hunters right now? I got the impression she hadn't been around much lately."

"Maybe—" Beth peered over his shoulder at the door "—maybe Scarlett was the target, but not for her anti-hunting stance."

"Then what? Her really creepy artwork?"

"The dream state ceremony last night."

Duke's pulse jumped. That would put Beth right back in the crosshairs since she'd participated, too. He rubbed his knuckles across his jaw. "Whoever placed that trap wants both you and Scarlett to stop looking into the

Timberline Trio case. Maybe they didn't care who they snared."

"What I don't understand is why me? Why is this person just warning me and not you? The FBI is investigating the Timberline Trio case, too."

"Because targeting the FBI is a bigger deal than scaring off some reporter and an artist playing at being a shaman."

She smacked his arm. "Scarlett's not playing at being a shaman—she is one."

"For all the good it did."

"It did help. You know I spoke to Dorothy Unger today."

"I got your text. Did she take you by the shoulders and proclaim that you looked just like Heather Brice?"

"Shh." Beth glanced at the open exam room door again. "She didn't, but she did tell me that quite a number of cabins in Timberline used to have red doors—seems it was a trend a while back."

"Those doors may no longer be red."

"I figured that, but she also gave me the name of a Realtor who might be able to help me figure out which cabins had the red doors. If I had that information, I could track down each one."

"Provided they're still standing. Not even the Brices' old home is still in existence."

"I know." She fell back against the table.

He hated to keep dashing her hopes, but she needed to get out of this town. The threats against her seemed to be getting more violent.

He smoothed a hand down her leg. Maybe he'd have some news for her shortly that would turn her away from this story and end this quest that seemed to be hazardous to her health.

The nurse bustled into the room. Touching the toe of Beth's mangled boot, she said, "Ruined a nice pair of boots, too. Let's get this off."

The nurse took a scalpel and sliced through the leather of the boot on Beth's calf. She peeled it off and clicked her tongue. "Your ankle is swollen for sure, but I don't see any blood. It doesn't look like the teeth of the trap made it to your flesh."

"I can't even imagine what that would've felt like." Beth shivered.

The nurse peeled off Beth's heavy sock and Beth grunted. "That looks bad."

"Swollen and the start of some massive bruising."

Duke leaned over and inspected Beth's injured ankle. "Is it broken?"

"The doctor will probably order some X-rays." The nurse ran some antiseptic towelettes over Beth's ankle and foot. "How's the pain on a scale from one to ten, ten being childbirth?"

A red tide crested in Beth's cheeks. "I've never experienced childbirth, but I'd put this pain at a six now— definitely a nine when it first happened."

The nurse held out a small cup with two green gel caps in it. "I'm going to give you a few ibuprofens for the pain and the swelling. The doctor may prescribe some stronger painkillers for you."

A doctor poked her head into the room. "I'm Dr. Thallman. There's a sheriff's deputy here to see you, but we're going to take you over to get some X-rays right now."

"I'll talk to the deputy." Duke leaned over and cupped Beth's face with one hand. "I'm not going anywhere."

He watched as they wheeled Beth away and then went to the waiting room, where Deputy Stevens was talking to the woman at the front desk.

"Stevens, Beth's getting some X-rays." He shook the deputy's hand.

"We have a couple of officers scanning the area in front of Scarlett Easton's place. They already found another trap, closer to the cabin."

Duke pinched the bridge of his nose. "What a sick joke. Any way to trace those traps?"

"Probably not." He swept his hat from his head. "But if we find out who's playing games like this, not only will he never get a hunting license in the state of Washington again, but we'll send him to jail."

"Do you think it's related to Scarlett's war with the hunters?" Duke's jaw hardened. If only he could believe that himself.

"Maybe, but we're not going to rule out Beth's mission here in Timberline. There still are a lot of folks here who are uneasy about the Timberline Trio case getting rehashed again—and let's just say Bill Raney is a hunter."

"I thought you cleared him of the other...pranks."

"We're going to start looking at everyone more closely."

Scarlett Easton burst through the emergency room doors. "Where's Beth? Is she okay?"

"Getting X-rays." Duke pointed at Stevens. "Did you hear they found another trap on your property?"

"I did. Maybe one for me and one for her."

Stevens asked, "You don't have anything to do with Beth's Timberline investigation, do you?"

"Me?" Scarlett drove a finger into her chest. "Not a chance."

A nurse poked her head out of the swinging doors leading to the exam rooms. "Beth's doing fine. Dr. Thallman is looking at her X-rays if you want to come back now, Deputy Stevens."

Duke brought up the rear behind Stevens and Scarlett as the nurse led them to the examination room.

Beth looked up from examining the pink wrap on her foot and ankle. "Pretty, isn't it?"

Scarlett tripped into the room and put an arm around Beth. "I'm so sorry."

"It's not your fault, Scarlett."

"My cabin seems to be bad luck for you."

"It could've just as easily been you caught in that trap."

Stevens cleared his throat. "One of those traps—we found another one."

Beth's mouth dropped open. "Oh, my God. If that one hadn't gotten me, the other one could've done the job."

"And the other one was bigger, could've caused more damage."

"It's a good thing I bought those heavy boots for this trip."

Dr. Thallman squeezed into the crowded room. "It is a good thing. Those boots probably saved you from breaking any bones."

"My foot's not broken?"

"Badly bruised and the bone is bruised as well. Keep

it wrapped, keep it elevated and I'm prescribing some painkillers if you need them." The doctor scribbled on a prescription pad and ripped it off.

"Is she okay to leave?" Duke took the prescription from the doctor.

"She is."

Stevens dragged a chair next to the examination table. "Before you leave, I'd like to ask you a few questions, Beth."

"We'll let you talk." Duke took Scarlett's arm. "I'll be in the waiting room, Beth."

When they reached the waiting room, Scarlett slouched on a vinyl chair. "I'm not staying in my cabin tonight. I'd been planning on leaving for Seattle tomorrow and then taking a flight to San Francisco for a friend's show. I can't help Beth anymore."

"You've done plenty."

She glanced at him sharply. "I just need to go back to the cabin to pack, and then I'll spend the night with my granny on the rez. Jason's driving me to Seattle."

"If something comes up, we can reach you on the cell phone number you gave Beth?"

"Yeah. Let me know when it's safe to return to my cabin."

Deputy Stevens caught the tail end of their conversation as he walked into the waiting room. "We have a couple of deputies canvassing your place, Scarlett. If we find anything else, we'll let you know."

"And if I remember anything else, I'll let you know, Quentin."

An orderly pushed Beth into the waiting room in a wheelchair.

Duke crouched beside her. "Can you walk on that ankle?"

She tipped her head at the orderly, holding a pair of crutches. "I'll have some crutches to get around at first, but once the swelling subsides a little more I should be fine."

The orderly handed the crutches to Duke and disappeared behind the swinging doors.

"We'll let you know if we discover anything else, too, Beth." Stevens clapped his hat onto his head. "Good night, all."

"Stevens? Scarlett's going back to her place to pack. Maybe it's a good idea if the deputies stay there until she leaves."

"I'll tell them."

When he left, Scarlett turned to Beth. "What did you want to see me about, anyway?"

"Oh, my God, I almost forgot." Beth pressed three fingers against her forehead. "The woman you saw with the strawberry blond hair in the vision—could she have been me as an adult, as I am now?"

"I don't know. Like Duke said, I'm not great at interpretation. I didn't get the impression that she was you. Why do you ask?"

"I spoke with someone who knew the Brices, and Patty Brice never had strawberry blond hair."

"I never said the woman was Patty Brice. I just don't know. I'm sorry, Beth. I can't help you anymore." Scarlett caught her bottom lip between her teeth. "What I haven't said yet to you or to Quentin Stevens is that the trap could've been a warning from my own people."

"The Quileute? Why?" Beth's eyes widened.

"They wouldn't want me talking about Dask'iya or the Timberline Trio case. I told you that before. The tribe doesn't discuss it."

"Would they really go that far to warn you?" Duke asked.

"It's a possibility. I just know I need to get away." She grabbed Beth's hand. "And you should, too."

"Thank you. I've been telling her that for a few days now."

"That's two to one, Beth. Find yourself another story. The Timberline kidnappings have been nothing but tragedy for everyone involved for as long as I can remember."

Beth squeezed Scarlett's hand. "Thanks for your concern, and thanks for all your help. I'm trying to reach a Realtor right now who can help me track down the red doors."

Scarlett rolled her eyes at Duke. "She's not going to listen, is she?"

"Don't worry. I plan to keep working on her. Are you okay if we leave now?"

"Yeah. You heard Quentin. The cops will probably still be wandering around my property when I get home."

Beth snapped her fingers. "My rental car is still at your place."

"You can't drive with that foot all wrapped up."

"Don't worry about it." Scarlett held up her hand. "I'll have Jason drive the car to your hotel and leave the keys at the front desk."

Duke dragged Beth's keys from his pocket and handed them to Scarlett. "Have a good trip."

They went to their separate cars, Beth awkwardly negotiating the crutches.

As he helped her into the SUV, he asked, "Did I hear you say you called the Realtor already?"

"Called her after my X-rays and left her a voice mail. If she's free for dinner, do you want to join us?"

"How could I possibly miss the discussion about cabins with red doors? Of course. And you're going to need some guidance before you get used to those crutches."

The drive back to the hotel was a quiet one. He was done trying to convince her to give up on this story. He knew one surefire way to do it, and if Mick would ever get back to him, it would be a done deal.

As he pulled into a parking spot, Beth's phone rang. She answered and he exited the car and leaned against the hood to wait.

When she got out, she held up her phone. "Dinner with Rebecca Geist at Sutter's tonight at seven. You in?"

"I'll be there." As she joined him, he took her by the shoulders before they entered the hotel. "I almost lost it when I saw you on the ground, that trap biting into your foot."

Her frame trembled beneath his hands. "It was… terrifying. The sound it made… Ugh. I'm going to hear that sound in my nightmares."

"What's it gonna take for you, Beth?"

"To leave Timberline? The truth. I'm going to leave Timberline when I discover the truth about my identity. Otherwise, what do I have?"

"You have me." He sealed his lips over hers and drew her close, burying one hand in her silky hair.

She melted against him for a moment, her mouth pliant against his. But then she broke away and stepped back.

"I just don't think you understand what this means to me, Duke. It's a lifetime of questions and doubts coming to a head in one corner of the world—right here. All my questions have led me here."

"You don't know, Beth. It's based on feelings and suppositions and red doors and frogs."

"And that's a start."

He closed his eyes and took a deep breath. He didn't want to take that all away from her—the hope, but he'd snatch it all away in a heartbeat to keep her safe.

"Okay. We have at least an hour before we have to leave for dinner. I'm going to take a shower. I'll stop by your room at around six forty-five."

She grabbed the front of his shirt. "Thanks for not pushing it, Duke."

Did she mean the topic of her identity or the kiss? Because he'd wanted to push both—especially the kiss.

AN HOUR LATER they drove into town and got a table for three at Sutter's. Beth had interviewed almost everyone she'd contacted, except for Jordan Young and a few others. As Beth had limped to their table, a few patrons glanced at her quickly, glanced away and then whispered among each other. Her reception in the dining room had cooled off compared to that first night.

Had the pranks and threats that had dogged her made the rounds and turned people off?

His gaze shifted to Beth studying the menu and his

stomach sank. She didn't care how chilly the reception. She had a goal and to hell with anything and anyone who stood in her way—including him.

A flashy blonde entered the restaurant and made a beeline to their table. "Beth St. Regis? I'd recognize you anywhere."

Duke stood up and pulled out her chair as Beth made the introductions. "Nice to meet you, Rebecca. This is Special Agent Duke Harper."

She shook his hand before taking a seat. "Now, aren't you the gentleman? These lumberjack types out here could learn a thing or two from a city boy like you."

Chloe was their waitress again and practically skipped to their table. "Jason told me someone had set some bear traps outside Scarlett's cabin and you stepped on one."

"Yeah, that happened." Beth lifted her wrapped foot in the air.

"That's crazy. Scarlett needs to stop ticking off those hunters."

"Did Scarlett get off to Seattle okay?"

Chloe nodded. "They're on their way. Jason texted me about an hour ago when they left. Can I get you guys some drinks?"

Rebecca ordered a glass of merlot while Beth got some hot tea. "I just took a couple of painkillers. If I mixed those with alcohol, I'd probably fall asleep at the table."

"I'll have that local brew on tap."

When Chloe walked away, Rebecca planted her elbows on the table and turned to Beth. "So, tell me everything. What secrets are you discovering about our little town?"

"Unfortunately the secrets seem to be piling up, and I don't have a clue."

"I heard what happened in here the other night between you and Bill Raney."

"His name keeps coming up, but since that initial threat from him, I haven't seen him at all." Beth glanced at the bar. "I don't think he's the only one who doesn't want me poking around."

Rebecca waved her manicured fingers. "Believe me, honey, the Timberline Trio case is the least of Bill's problems." She winked. "I'm his biggest problem right now."

Duke put his phone on vibrate and tucked it into the front pocket of his shirt. "You're taking away his business?"

"There was nothing to take away. I'm earning business and he's not—maybe if he'd lay off the booze."

"I heard from Dorothy Unger that you were the best, and that's why I called you."

Chloe stopped by with their drinks and they ordered their food while they had her attention.

"I helped Dot get out of her old house when her husband passed away and got her into a newer, smaller place." She folded her hands. "So, tell me how I can help you."

"Dorothy mentioned that there was a trend toward red doors for Timberline cabins a long time ago. Would you know which cabins had the red doors?"

Rebecca blinked her false lashes. "Red doors. Red doors. Not many of those cabins left."

"Are there some left?" Beth hunched forward, rattling her teacup.

"There are a couple, but I'm not sure if they're the original red-door cabins or if they're newly painted. I'm going to have to do a little research. I have a lot of archive photos of the cabins in Timberline. I'm sure I can find some of them."

"That would be great, Rebecca, and if you point me in the right direction, I can help you do the research."

Duke's phone buzzed in his pocket. He slipped it out and cupped it in his hand. When he saw that Mick had sent him a text, a muscle jumped in his jaw.

"Is that work?"

"Yeah. I'm just going to step outside for a minute, if you ladies will excuse me."

Rebecca patted Beth's arm. "True gentleman, that one."

Duke pushed back from the table and tried not to run out of the restaurant. When he got to the sidewalk, he was panting like he'd just run a marathon.

He entered his code to unlock his phone and swiped his finger across the display. The blood rushed to his head when he read Mick's text and he braced one hand against the wall of the building to steady himself.

He placed a call to Mick. When Mick picked up, Duke said, "You're sure?"

"DNA doesn't lie, my brother, even on a rush job like this one. Is it going to help solve the case?"

"I think so."

"I have to get off the phone. It's late here and I'm helping my son with his math homework."

"Just wanted to verify. Thanks, buddy."

Duke strolled back into the restaurant. He didn't know how he was going to get through the rest of this meal.

When he got to the table, Rebecca was telling Beth all about her wedding plans.

She tapped her head. "Of course, it's all up here right now since my fiancé hasn't actually committed to a date yet."

"Nothing wrong with a long engagement, really get to know someone."

"What about you two?" Rebecca flicked her finger back and forth between him and Beth. "Any wedding plans?"

Beth's cup clattered into her saucer. "Oh, we're not… we're not together."

"Oops." Rebecca put two fingers to her lips. "I'm usually pretty good at things like that."

Duke grabbed Beth's hand. "We were together—once."

"You see? I knew it. I can always tell."

Beth tilted her head at him, a half smile on her lips.

Hadn't he made it clear he'd like to pick up where they'd left off? She'd been the one pushing him away. The night he'd told her he'd made a mistake two years ago had been the night she'd cooled down toward him. If a relationship came too easily for Beth, she'd probably dismiss it as unworthy of her efforts. She liked the struggle. It was what she knew.

Their dinner arrived and Rebecca did her part to keep the conversation going between bites of food. Thank God for talkative real-estate agents.

As they were finishing up, Bill Raney came into the restaurant with a few buddies, including Jordan Young, and bellied up to the bar.

Rebecca narrowed her eyes. "Honestly, Bill wouldn't

have the guts to go sneaking through the forest laying bear traps for unsuspecting women. I wouldn't worry too much about him."

Duke asked, "I gather he's not your biggest fan. Has he ever bothered you?"

"You know, come to think of it…" Rebecca tapped her long nails together. "Someone sabotaged a couple of my open houses last month."

"Bill the Prankster strikes again?" Beth turned her head to take in the group at the bar.

Jordan Young waved her over.

She smiled and stuck out her bandaged foot. "At least Jordan won't think I'm too chicken to go up to Raney."

Young pushed away from the bar and drew up the fourth chair at the table. "Do you mind?"

Rebecca waved her finger at him. "As long as you give me a shot at your next listing, Jordan."

"I'm loyal to my friends, Rebecca, but I admire your success from afar." He tapped the table in front of Beth. "What happened to your foot?"

"I'm shocked you haven't heard yet."

"I've been fishing most of the day. What did I miss?"

"Someone set some bear traps in front of Scarlett Easton's place and I got stuck in one."

"Damn. Did you break it?"

"Just bruised it."

"Scarlett okay?"

"She's fine. Left town for a few weeks."

Jordan tsked. "That's no way to solve a disagreement over hunting. I'll talk to the mayor about cracking down."

"I'm sure Scarlett would appreciate that."

"How about you, Agent Harper? Any luck cracking the cold case?"

"We're investigating a few leads. They're not called 'cold cases' for nothing."

"And you're involved how, Rebecca?"

"I'll never tell. Maybe Beth just wants to buy some property after experiencing the beauty and serenity of the area."

Duke smothered his snort. Timberline had been anything but serene for Beth.

"Well, she's consulting the best." He rapped his knuckles on the table. "You folks enjoy your evening. And, Beth, I should be around for the next few days if you are."

"I'll be here. I'll try calling your office again to schedule something."

He took a card from his card case and called to Chloe. "Do you have a pen, sweetheart?"

She smacked a pen on the table and spun away.

Young scribbled something on one of his cards. "Here's my direct line, Beth. Give me a call when you're ready to interview me."

"Thanks, Jordan."

He sauntered back to his friends at the bar and a hard stare from Raney.

Maybe Bill Raney wasn't the hapless drunk everyone thought he was.

Chloe returned to the table with the check. "Sorry for

the delay. I wasn't coming back with Mr. Young here. He can get handsy, if you know what I mean."

"Honey, at my age handsy isn't necessarily a bad thing." Rebecca laughed as she tried to grab the check from Chloe.

Beth was faster. "This is a tax-deductible dinner expense for me. You're going to help me find those red-door cabins, aren't you?"

"I'm going to do my damnedest. Now, if you don't mind, I'm going to scoot out of here and get back to the office to wrap up a few things."

When she left the restaurant after flitting to about five tables on her way out, Duke wiped the back of his hand across his forehead. "Whew. She's a dynamo."

"And efficient. I have complete faith in her to find those red doors."

Duke stroked her arm. "Let me get you back to the hotel and tuck you into bed. Maybe you can pop a few more of those painkillers and get a good night's sleep."

"You're being awfully…handsy tonight."

"I just want to take care of you, Beth." He laced his fingers with hers. "Do you believe me?"

"I believe you, and do you believe me when I say I just want the truth?"

"I can help you with that, too, Beth." He tugged on her hand. "Let's get out of here."

She leaned on him while she adjusted her crutches beneath her arms, and with a nod to Jordan, she navigated through the tables while Duke ran interference.

When they got back to the hotel, he followed her into

her room. "I meant that about tucking you in. Do you want me to run you a bath?"

"I'd probably fall asleep in the tub and drown, but if you want to wait in here while I get ready for bed in case I topple over in the bathroom, that would be great."

"I'm your man in case of toppling." He stretched out on the bed and grabbed the remote control to the TV.

She gathered a few items and retreated to the bathroom.

While she ran the water and banged around in there, he ran a few lines through his head. He could put everything to rest tonight.

She emerged from the bathroom in her flannel pajamas and hopping without her crutches.

He jumped from the bed to help her. "Don't put any pressure on that foot yet."

She dropped some clothes in her suitcase. "I'm fine."

He pulled back the covers and helped her into bed. He wanted to crawl right in after her, but first things first.

She plumped up her pillows and eased back against them. "Aaah, this feels good."

"Do you need any more meds?"

"Not until after midnight. If the pain wakes me up, I'll take a few more."

He filled a glass with water from the tap and put her pill bottle on the nightstand. "For midnight."

"Thanks, Duke. You've been a big help."

"I'm going to be an even bigger help, Beth. I have something important to tell you."

Her face grew still. "What is it?"

He sat next to her on the bed and took both of her hands in his. "You're not Heather Brice."

Chapter Thirteen

She jerked away from Duke, banging her head on the headboard. His touch felt heavy, oppressive, and she snatched her hands away from his. "Why are you saying that? Why are you trying to discourage me?"

"It's more than that, Beth." He tried to take her hand again but she folded her arms and tucked her hands beneath her elbows. "I have proof."

Her tongue felt like sandpaper as she licked her lips. "How could you have proof? What did you do?"

"I requested a sample of the Brices' DNA through the FBI labs."

She clamped her hands over her ears as if that could stop the truth coming from Duke's lips. Bending at the waist, she touched her forehead to her knees. The pieces of her carefully constructed future began crashing down around her—the happy reunion, the loving family, her place in the world.

Duke's hand on her back felt like a lead weight, but she didn't have the energy to shrug him off. A black hole had sucked her into its vortex and she was spinning and spinning with no sense of time or place, no anchor.

"I'm sorry, Beth. I couldn't stand to see you twisting

yourself into knots over this, putting yourself into need-less danger." He swept aside the curtain of hair shield-ing her face. "I didn't cause the Brices any anguish. I didn't tell them about your suspicions. I let them know the FBI was working the cold case and needed their DNA. I ran it against yours from some strands of your hair and...no match."

A tear ran down her cheek and she let it drop off the edge of her chin. She managed a hoarse whisper from her tight throat. "Why did you do that? Why didn't you tell me?"

"The bigger question, Beth, is why didn't you ask me to do that? Your excuse for not going straight to the Brices was that you wanted to spare their feelings in case nothing came of your claim, but you always knew the FBI could request their DNA without arousing any suspicions. The fact that we'd taken this case out of mothballs made it easy."

She raised her head and another tear slipped down her face. "You know why."

"You were afraid of the answer. You were afraid of the truth." Duke caught her next tear on the pad of his thumb. "I get that. It's why I didn't tell you I was or-dering the DNA."

"I knew." She rubbed her nose against the sheet cov-ering her knees. "I saw a text from Mickey the other night about the Brices. I knew you were up to some-thing. I just couldn't figure out why you wouldn't tell me what."

"Ah, that was it." He ran a hand down her leg and traced the edge of the heavy wrap around her ankle. "Maybe I should've told you, but then you would've been on pins and needles waiting for the results and if the results had been different..."

Falling back against the pillows, she said, "You're glad they're not different. You're relieved I'm not Heather Brice."

"I want you to be happy, Beth." He shoved a hand through his thick hair and left it there, holding the side of his head. "I knew you'd been building up this perfect life with the Brices, envisioning them as the all-American family, a place for you to fit in at last. God, I want that for you, Beth, but you can have that with me. We can have it together. I'm looking for my perfect family, too."

A sob racked her body and she covered her face with her hands. "You can't have that with me. I can't help you create that perfect family because I'm broken. I'm damaged."

The mattress sank as Duke climbed next to her on the bed. He wrapped one arm around her shoulders and pulled her against his chest. "Don't say that. You're the most perfect woman I know—the girl of my adolescent fantasies come to life in living, strawberry blond color."

Taking a long, shuddering breath, she squirmed out of his hold. She grabbed handfuls of his shirt and pulled him close. "You don't know. I've already destroyed any family we could have together."

He touched his forehead to hers and smoothed the hair from her damp face. "I told you, Beth. I understand why you deceived me two years ago. I understand you."

"You don't know me."

"I didn't know you before. I saw you as the untouchable girl of my dreams, perfect in every way. Now I see the human woman that you are, with all your flaws and insecurities, and I still love you. I love you more."

She squeezed her eyes shut and ran her fingers across his rough beard. She'd been waiting so long to hear those words from him...and now she'd have to fling them back in his face.

"I don't deserve your love. I tricked you again. I deceived you." She pulled away from him so she could look into his dark eyes and see the love fade away. "I had a miscarriage. I lost your baby, Duke."

His eyes widened for a split second and grew darker as his pupils dilated. "When?"

"I found out I was pregnant when I got back to LA from Chicago—about three weeks after."

"What happened?"

"This is what happened." She slammed a fist against her gut. "Me. I happened. Unfit for a family."

"Stop it." His fingers pinched into her shoulders. "Tell me what happened to our baby, Beth."

"I don't know. I had the miscarriage just a few weeks after I discovered the pregnancy. It all came and went so fast, it felt like a dream."

She gritted her teeth and braced herself for Duke's anger, for his accusations. She welcomed them. Deserved them.

His hold on her shoulders melted into a caress and he dragged her back into his arms again, tucking her head against the curve of his neck. "I'm sorry you were alone when it happened. I should've been there for you."

"Don't you get it, Duke?" She sniffled. "I didn't even tell you about the pregnancy. I probably never would've told you about the baby."

"I don't believe that for a minute." He rubbed a circle on her back. "You would've told me. You never would've allowed our baby to grow up without knowing his or her father. Whatever your feelings for me were at the time, you would've recognized the value of giving our child a father. I know that about you...now."

"But it's over. I lost the baby."

"Did the doctor indicate that you'd have problems in the future? Was there a reason why you miscarried?"

His heart pounded beneath her cheek and she smoothed her hand over his chest. "No problems. He said it's something that happens in the first trimester sometimes."

"Then it wasn't your fault and you can get pregnant again." He kissed her temple. "You can have that family, Beth. You don't need the Brices. You don't need the Kings. All you need is me. And I sure as hell need you."

He wedged his thumb beneath her chin and tilted up her head. He traced the tracks of her tears with his fingertip until he'd dried them all, and then he kissed her lips. They throbbed beneath the gentle pressure of his mouth.

Between the kisses he planted along the line of her jaw, he whispered, "I. Want. You. More. Than. Anything."

"Duke, is this coming from pity?" She cupped his jaw in her hand, the stubble of his beard tickling her palm. "Because I'm okay now. I'm sorry I broke down. In fact, I—"

"Shh." He put a finger against her lips. Then he took her hand and guided it between his legs. "Does this feel like pity to you?"

She stroked his erection through the denim of his

jeans. It felt like a visit to the candy store and a two-point rating share all rolled up into one big treat.

He growled and unbuttoned his fly. She took the obvious hint and peeled back his jeans while shoving her hand beneath the waistband of his black briefs.

The growl turned into a groan as she teased his flesh with her fingernails and kissed his mouth. He deepened the kiss and tugged at her pajama top, pulling it over her head.

He cupped one bare breast with his hand, dragging his thumb across her peaked nipple. She gasped against his lips and he shifted his mouth to the top of her breast. He kissed a circle around her nipple before sucking it into his mouth.

She arched her back, giving him more, her hips rocking forward, her hand stroking his hard-on.

She unbuttoned his shirt and rolled up his T-shirt, exposing his tight abs. She ran the flat of her hand along the ridges and then ducked her head and pressed a kiss in the middle, his skin warm against her lips.

Yanking on the edge of the shirt, she said, "That's the problem with cold weather—too many clothes."

"Sort of heightens the anticipation, don't you think?" He slipped off her pajama bottoms with one fluid motion.

"Says the man who has just a flimsy pair of pajamas to dispense with."

"There's still these." He ran a finger along the elastic of her bikini underwear clinging to her hips.

"What are you waiting for?"

He pulled down the panties and the silky material

skimmed over her thighs. "This is a little more difficult. I'll try to be careful."

He inched the underwear over her knees and gently tugged them past her bandage. His gaze swept across her body, leaving tingles in its wake.

"Nothing but a pink bandage—incredibly sexy."

She wiggled her toes and rolled to her side. "You can get naked now."

He shed the rest of his clothing in record time and stretched out beside her again. He pressed his body against hers, along every line, and she let his warmth seep into her skin.

For a moment she let everything slip away—all the heartache and disappointment. She had her man by her side again and there were no secrets between them.

He followed her spine with one knuckle and caressed her derriere, fitting her against his body, his erection prodding between her thighs.

He traced over the rest of her body, as if drawing it from scratch. Could he recreate her? Make her whole?

His touch gave her goose bumps, made her believe anything was possible. He finished his exercise with a kiss on her mouth. Then he pressed her back against the pillows.

"I'm going to make you feel better than any painkiller in the entire pharmacy." He knelt between her legs and flattened his hands against the insides of her thighs. Lifting her injured leg, he rested it on his shoulder. "The doc said to keep it elevated, right?"

"That's one way to do it."

When his lips brushed her sensitive flesh, her eyes

fluttered closed and her fingers burrowed into his hair. He circled with his tongue and then plunged it inside her.

She let out a long sigh, but then the tension began to build like a hot coil in her belly. Her fingernails dug into his scalp as he teased her higher and higher.

Her climax broke her apart into a million little pieces. All the anxiety and fear that had been building up since she'd started this quest shattered. She wouldn't let it take hold of her again.

Duke slid her leg from his shoulder. "Okay?"

"Mmm, more than okay and ready for you. Really ready for you this time, Duke. No more games."

"Nothing between us." He rose to his knees and she wrapped her fingers around his erection.

"Like one."

Bracing his hands on either side of her head, he drove inside her. A spasm of pleasure flashed across his face.

She clawed at the hard muscle of his buttocks, hooking her good leg around his hips, urging him deeper.

His rhythm was erratic, as if the tumult of his senses had overwhelmed him and he'd forgotten for a moment how a man loved a woman.

She touched his face. Their eyes met. He shivered and slowed his pace, plunging into her deeply and pulling out just enough to make it feel like coming home when he returned to her.

As his thrusts grew bolder and faster, she pressed her lips against his warm flesh, baring her teeth against his collarbone.

He moaned, a sound of such pure pleasure it made her toes curl. On the very next thrust, he exploded inside her. He sank to his forearms and took possession of her mouth. The motion of his kiss mimicked the waves of his orgasm and he didn't stop kissing her until he was spent inside her.

He hoisted himself off her body. "How's your foot?"

Her lips curled into a smile. "My foot had nothing to do with any of that."

"Is it feeling left out?" He slid to the bottom of the bed and kissed each of her toes sticking out of the bandage.

"Did you develop a foot fetish when we were apart?"

"I have a fetish for every part of your body. Don't you know that? I could worship your elbow and count myself lucky."

She crooked her index finger. "I have to admit I'm partial to one part of your body in particular."

"My brain, right?" He settled beside her again and scooped her into a hug, rubbing the gooseflesh from her arms.

"That's it." She kissed his chiseled jawline. "And that didn't feel like pity sex at all."

"As a man, that's the best way I know how to offer comfort. But pity? I don't pity you. So, you're not Heather Brice with the perfect family waiting for you at the end of the rainbow. I knew my family, knew where I came from—and it wasn't perfect. Maybe the Brices aren't perfect, either. You'll weather the storm."

"You're right. The news about the Brices' DNA was just a hiccup."

"I meant what I said, Beth." He massaged the back of her neck. "As long as I'm stuck in cold-case hell, I can turn you on to a few good stories."

"That would be great once I'm done here."

"Not that I won't miss you, but I can drive you to Seattle and you can get on the next plane to LA. I'll have to stay here, of course, but I'm sure Mick won't mind if I take a few weekends off and head to LA."

"I'm not leaving right away, Duke."

"You don't need to pretend with anyone. I'll make sure word gets out that your producer cut the story or you felt you didn't have enough to create a compelling enough episode of *Cold Case Chronicles*."

"I mean—" she pulled the sheet up to her chin, her heart thumping "—I'm not giving up here."

The massage stopped. "What does that mean? You don't have anything on the Timberline Trio. There's no story for you here."

She sat up, adjusting the pillow behind her back. "I don't care about the Timberline Trio case, especially now that I'm not involved in it at all."

His dark brows collided over his nose. "I don't understand. What is there for you in Timberline?"

"What was always here—my true identity. I may not be Heather Brice or Kayla Rush, but the secret to my origin is here in Timberline. And I'm going to stay here until I discover it."

Chapter Fourteen

A chill stole over Duke's flesh, still damp with the exertion of making love. He rolled away from Beth and planted his feet on the carpet. "You can't be serious."

"*You* can't be serious to believe I'd give up now that I'm so close."

"Close to what? For whatever reason, a person or persons unknown to you does not want you poking around Timberline, and as long as you continue to do so, your life is in danger."

"I don't give a damn what the people of Timberline want. I know my past lies here and I'm going to solve the mystery of my identity if it's the last thing I do."

"It just might be."

She flicked her fingers in the air. "There have been some warnings, but nothing life-threatening."

He smacked his forehead. "Someone shot at you."

"He missed. Do you really think an experienced hunter would miss his prey?"

"We don't know that the person shooting at you is an experienced hunter, and I'm sure hunters miss all the time." He fell back on the bed so that his head was in her lap. "Beth, it's not worth it. You don't know what you're looking for."

"I'm looking for a cabin with a red door and two birds somewhere. If I can trace the property records for that cabin, maybe I can find out who had it twenty-five years ago and discover what happened there."

"I'm in awe of your…"

"Brilliance?" She combed her fingers through his hair.

"Stubbornness." He captured her fingers. "What if you do discover your true family? They may not be the loving family the Brices were. The Brices had their child stolen from them. Your family gave you away and didn't want to be traced. I'm not gonna stand by and watch you get devastated by the discovery."

"I…I'm not going to be devastated. It is what it is. I just want to know at this point. Wouldn't you?"

"I would." He pressed a kiss against the center of her palm. "I just don't want to see you hurt—physically or emotionally. You're back in my life now, Beth, and I don't want to lose you again."

"Stand by me. Stay with me. If you're going to be my family, then that's what it takes." She leaned forward and kissed his forehead. "I'm tired of secrets, Duke. I want a fresh start with you, a clean slate before we… do whatever it is we're going to do."

"If you're going to stay here in Timberline, I'll be with you. I'm not going to let you run off looking for red doors by yourself."

"I was hoping you'd say that because I don't think I can do this by myself. I'm better with you, Duke."

"I just hope you don't get hurt."

"If I do, I know you'll have my back."

"Count on it." He slid off the bed and swept her card

key from the nightstand. "I'm going to my own room to brush my teeth, but I'll be back."

She snuggled against the pillow and closed her eyes. "I'll be waiting."

When Duke returned to his room he punched a pillow. He hadn't been happy when the Brices' DNA didn't match Beth's, but he'd been relieved. He'd figured she'd give up on Timberline and go back to LA, but she felt some connection to this place. He had to trust her instincts.

He brushed his teeth and splashed some water on his face. He pulled on a pair of running shorts and returned to Beth's room.

The TV flickered in the darkness and he crept over to her bed. She'd fallen asleep on her back with her foot propped up on pillows beneath the covers.

He dropped his shorts and slid between the sheets, next to her. She hadn't bothered putting her pajamas back on and he rolled to his side to press his body against her nakedness.

She murmured something through parted lips and he kissed the corner of her mouth. Beth had no intention of giving up her search, and whatever happened, he'd be there for the fallout.

THE NEXT MORNING after breakfast, he and Beth joined Rebecca in her office. She led them to a conference room and flipped open her laptop. She eyed Duke over the top of her computer. "This isn't part of the FBI investigation, is it?"

He held up his hands. "I'm off duty today. Would it make a difference?"

"I just don't want to get subpoenaed or have our records called into evidence."

"This is for the show only. You don't even have to be on camera if you don't want to be."

"Well, I wouldn't mind that as long as you get a shot of my sign out front. Unless—" she powered up her computer "—the story ends up driving potential buyers away from Timberline."

Beth shrugged off her down vest. "The case was twenty-five years ago. I don't see how that's going to affect Timberline's reputation. If anything, Wyatt Carson already did that by trying to play the hero."

As she typed on her keyboard, Rebecca gave an exaggerated shiver. "That was creepy, but I still managed to get a good price for Kendall Rush's house."

Duke cleared his throat. "What are you going to look up this morning?"

"I have access to all of Timberline's old housing records, along with some pictures. With any luck, I should be able to identify several of the homes with the red doors."

"Let's get started." Beth scooted her chair closer to the table and leaned over Rebecca's arm.

Rebecca's fingers flew over the keyboard. "Let's see. Twenty years ago, twenty-five, not much construction during that period. Thirty, thirty-five. Now we're getting somewhere."

Beth leaned forward, poking at the screen. "This is new construction for that time period?"

"Yes. I can click on the photos for this bunch."

A cabin filled the computer screen, but it didn't have a red door.

Beth slumped back in her chair. "That's not one."

"Let me click through these photos." Each time Rebecca tapped her keyboard, a new cabin popped up on the screen. None had red doors.

"There's another grouping. I'm going to close out this bunch." She launched another set of photos and Beth sucked in a breath when the first one appeared.

"This is it." Beth practically bounced in her chair. "These are the cabins."

Rebecca brought up the cabins one by one and each cabin sported a red front door.

Duke counted the red-door cabins aloud until she came to the end. "That's eight cabins with red doors. Do you recognize any of them, Rebecca?"

"I thought I recognized a couple." She minimized the window and brought up another application. "I'm going to copy and paste the cabin addresses in here to get their locations and to see if they still exist."

An hour later Rebecca printed out a list of five red-door cabins that were still standing. The other three had been demolished.

"You are the best." Beth plucked the pages from the printer. "If I ever know of anyone moving to this area, I will send them your way."

"Just give me a plug on your show." She squinted at her laptop. "I have to get ready for my open house. Have fun investigating, and if you annoy anyone by poking around, don't tell them I sent you."

When they got into Duke's SUV, Beth smoothed out the paper on her lap. "GPS?"

"Plug in all of them and we'll try to hit them in order of location."

Beth tapped in the address of each of the cabins on the list and they designed a route so they wouldn't be backtracking.

Duke turned the key in the ignition and glanced at Beth. "What's your plan? Are you going to invite yourself into someone's home, stand in the middle of the room and tell them you're waiting for a psychic experience?"

"I'm not sure yet. I'll figure it out when I get there."

"Okay, it's your rodeo. I'm just the technical adviser...and the bodyguard."

She squeezed his bicep. "I like the sound of that."

They drove out to the first two cabins, which resided on the same street. Civilization had encroached on the wilderness in this area as a wide, paved road cut through the forest, giving the houses on this street manicured backyards bordering the forest edge.

Duke parked his car on the street in front of the first cabin and looked at Beth. "What now?"

"I...I'm going to get out and walk around. Maybe I'll knock on the front door and pretend I'm looking for someone."

"Yeah, because you're not totally recognizable in this town by now."

"I could use that to my advantage." She unbuckled her seat belt and reached into his backseat. "I'll take my video camera. I was filming areas before."

"Let's do it."

He went around to the passenger side to get Beth's door.

She looked up from the camera in her lap. "Might

as well start filming now. In fact, this is a good way to get a record of each cabin."

He helped her out of the car. "Are you going to be able to hold the camera and navigate with your crutch?"

"I don't think so. Can you play cameraman for me?"

"Yeah, just don't tell Adam." He took the camera from her. "Where is your crew, anyway? Are they getting antsy?"

"They're working on something else right now. I already indicated to Scott that this segment might not be a go and to hold off sending them."

"All right, then." He held the camera in front of him and framed the cabin in the viewfinder. "Cabin number one in the red-door cabin follies."

Beth poked him with her crutch and then appeared in his frame. "I'm going to knock on the door."

He followed her to the porch and then the door swung open and a boy cannoned down the front porch, leaving the door standing wide behind him. He tripped to a stop when he saw them.

"Hi there. Do you live here?"

"Mom!"

"Tanner, close the door." A petite woman appeared at the doorway. She put a hand to her chest. "Oh, you scared me."

"Sorry." Beth flashed her pearly whites. "I'm doing a little filming in the area. Do you mind?"

"Oh, I know who you are."

"Mom, can I go to Joe's house now?"

"Go ahead." She crossed her arms and propped up the doorjamb with her shoulder. "This area doesn't have much to do with the Timberline Trio, and I didn't even live here then."

"I know that, but a few of these cabins were standing twenty-five years ago. I'm just getting a sense of the area back then."

"You can film outside the house if you want, but I don't have time to talk to you and if the dog starts barking you're going to have to leave."

"I understand. Thank you."

But the woman had slammed the door on Beth's thanks.

Duke shifted the camera to the side. "Ouch. She's not too interested in appearing on TV, is she?"

"No, but I'm not getting anything from this house anyway."

"Like, recognition?"

"Like, any kind of vibe."

"You're not Scarlett." He snapped the viewfinder closed. "You felt those things with her because she let you into her vision."

"She told me I had a particular sensitivity. That's why this landscape in Timberline, the forest, the greenery, sets me off. It always has."

He wasn't going to argue with her or convince her otherwise. He had a support role today and he planned to fulfill that role to the best of his ability. "On to cabin number two, then."

Cabin number two was similar to one—more like a house and inhabited with residents, none too eager to speak with Beth. Duke filmed the exterior for her, but this cabin didn't speak to her, either.

They had more luck with cabin number three. As

they drove up to the front of it, Beth sat up. "This looks spooky, doesn't it?"

"It looks abandoned."

"I'm getting the chills already." Beth stretched her arms out in front of her.

Duke cut the engine and hoisted the strap of the camera over his shoulder.

He filmed the front of the cabin as Beth hobbled up to the porch without her crutches. "Hello?"

Duke tried the door, but the rotting wood held firm. He picked at a chip of paint with his fingernail. "I think this still has the original red paint on the door."

"Seems to be locked up tight." Beth stepped off the porch steps. "I'm going to look around the side."

"Hang on." He put the camera down. "The landscaping, if you can call it that, is overgrown with weeds. Grab my arm."

Taking his arm, she leaned against him. He navigated a path through the tangled shrubs and turned the corner of the cabin. The wild brush of the forest grew close to the exterior cabin wall.

Beth tugged on his hand. "The window's broken."

They crept up to the shattered window and Duke dug for his phone. Poking his head inside the window, he turned on the phone's light and scanned the room.

"Do you see anything?"

"It's a big mess. Looks like animals, kids, transients or all three have been in here."

She yanked on the back of his shirt. "Let me have a look."

He backed away from the window and handed her

the phone. "It's too high for you to see inside, especially without cutting yourself on the jagged glass."

He scanned the ground and spotted a stump of wood. "This'll work."

He dragged the wood under the window and helped Beth stand on it, holding her around the waist. "Do you see anything that grabs you?"

"No, but it's creepy. I'd like to find out more about it."

"I'm sure Rebecca can help with that."

Duke filmed more of the cabin before they got back in the car. "Three down, two to go."

Beth checked her phone. "They're in the same general area, farther out in the boonies."

"Let's go and you can review my awesomely professional video later."

He swung off the main highway, down one of the many roads that branched into the forest. Cabins and small houses dotted the road. "I wonder when housing for the Evergreen employees is going to creep out this way."

"I think there's something about the zoning that doesn't permit certain types of housing."

"I'm sure Jordan Young is working on an angle for that right now."

"And he'll probably give all the work to his worthless buddy, Bill." She tapped her phone. "Oops. I think the GPS lost its way."

"We don't have too many choices here until we plunge into the forest." He pointed to a marker up ahead on the side of the road. "There's an access road there." When they reached the marker, he made the turn.

Beth's knees bounced and she wedged her hands beneath her thighs. "Reminds me of Scarlett's area."

"Remote and rugged. These must be hunting and fishing cabins."

Beth scooted forward in her seat, her back stiff.

"Are you okay?"

Her lips parted and her chest rose and fell rapidly.

"Beth? What's wrong?"

She cupped her hands around her nose and mouth and huffed out a breath. "Feeling a little anxious. I'll be fine."

The trees crowded in on them, shutting out the light of the afternoon. Mist clung to the windshield and he flipped on the wipers. "We can stop right here, turn around."

Shaking her head, she hugged herself. "It's that feeling, Duke. The forest is closing in on me, suffocating me."

"I'm turning around."

"No!" She grabbed the steering wheel. "I can do this. I can get through it."

They came across a path leading from the access road. "My guess is the first cabin's back there."

"Then we'd better take a look."

He parked and helped her from the car. "How about one crutch?"

"I'll try it." She tucked it under one arm and he held her other arm.

The cabin arose from a clearing. A walkway paved with natural stone cut a path through a neat garden.

"It looks inhabited." He squeezed her hand. "Still getting the feeling?"

The door burst open and a man stepped out onto the porch with a shotgun.

Beth stumbled and Duke caught her.

"You lost?"

"Can you put the gun down?" Duke curled his arm around Beth's body and felt a tremble roll through her frame.

"Oh, this?" He lowered the shotgun. "Just came out here to clean it. Didn't know anyone was here. Got myself a turkey this morning."

Beth found her voice. "Do you own this cabin?"

"No, ma'am. My name's Doug Johnson, if you want to check it out. I rent the cabin once a year to do some hunting—turkey mostly. The wife likes it if I can bring one home for the Thanksgiving dinner." He tugged on his hat. "Are you looking for the owner?"

"Who is it?" Duke asked.

"I rent it from some management company—Raney Realty."

Beth pinched his side. "Bill Raney?"

"Might be, but I deal with a woman." He jerked his thumb over his shoulder. "I think I have a card, if you want me to get it."

Duke waved. "That's okay. We can look them up in town. There another cabin out this way?"

"About a mile up the road."

"Is that one for rent, too?"

"I think it is, but there's nobody there now. It's not as nice as this one."

"Raney Realty have that one?"

"I think so. I keep coming back to this place, so I'm not sure."

"Thanks. Sorry to disturb you." Beth dug her crutch into the ground. "Four down, one to go."

When they got back in the car, Duke touched her icy cheek. "Are you sure you're okay?"

"Do you find it coincidental that the cabin giving me the heebie-jeebies is managed by Bill Raney?"

"Yep." Beth had regained her focus and he didn't even bother asking if she wanted to check out the last cabin. She was like a dog with a bone at this point.

He drove almost a mile up the road until he spied another path with a mailbox at its entrance.

He pulled off the road as far as he could and met Beth at the passenger door. Her pale face and shallow breathing indicated another panic attack was on the horizon.

"Can I get you something, Beth? We don't have to do this now, or you can wait in the car and I'll take the camera."

"It's so strong, Duke. I wish I had Scarlett with me."

"I'm with you." He handed her the crutch. "Let's go face this thing head-on."

He adjusted his gait to hers, his head swiveling from side to side, his body tense.

Beth fell against him with a cry as she pointed to the mailbox. "Look, two birds. Just like Scarlett said—two birds. This is the place."

Chapter Fifteen

Beth swayed, but Duke kept her steady. The uneasy feelings had been building in her gut as soon as Duke had turned down the access road. Now, standing in front of the mailbox, they overwhelmed her.

Breaking away from Duke, she staggered toward the mailbox and grabbed it. She traced her finger along the edges of the two birds that had been carved at the top of the mailbox. "This is what Scarlett saw."

He placed a hand against her back. "Are you ready to have a look?"

"You're not going to try to talk me out of it again?"

"You've come this far. There's no turning back."

Dragging in a breath, she leaned on her crutch. "Let's go."

A path wended its way toward the cabin, which was a duplicate of the one down the road. The hunter had been right. His rental was in better shape, but this one hadn't been abandoned.

They approached the front door, which was no longer red, and Duke took the two steps in one long stride. He banged on the solid wood door. "Hello? Anyone here?"

"I suppose we won't find any broken windows in this cabin." Beth hobbled around to the side.

The brush had been cleared away from the structure, creating a neat perimeter. Beth followed the outer wall of the cabin, the adrenaline pumping through her body. She pressed her forehead against one of the windows, but someone had tugged a pair of neat curtains across the glass.

She jumped as Duke put a hand on her shoulder. "Can't see inside this one, but this is it—the cabin of my nightmares. I'm sure of it, and the formerly red door and the two birds on the mailbox line up with Scarlett's vision."

"I doubt the owner of the cabin, especially if it's managed by Bill Raney, is going to allow us to just walk in and search around."

"Probably not. What if we rent the place?"

"Wouldn't that seem strange since you've been staying in the hotel all this time? And if Raney doesn't want you snooping around, I'm sure he could come up with a million reasons for the owner not to rent to you."

She traced a finger across the smooth glass. "I wonder who owns it. I really want to get inside."

"Can you get any reception out here? If you text Rebecca, she'll have the answer for you in a matter of minutes."

She pulled her phone from her pocket and tapped it. "No reception. That info is going to have to wait."

"But the rest doesn't have to wait." He brushed aside her hair and kissed the nape of her neck. "I'll be right back."

He headed to the back of the cabin and disappeared around the corner.

A wave of panic engulfed her again and she closed

her eyes and pressed her hand against the rough wood of the cabin wall. "Duke?"

"Right here."

Her lids flew open to find him beside her. "What did you find?"

"Whaddya know? Someone left the back door open."

"You broke in?"

"Shh. We're not going to steal anything. We're just looking around to see if it's suitable for renting."

"I'm gonna end up getting you fired over this."

He took her hand. "If I'm going to get fired, we might as well get something out of it."

The forest edged up pretty closely to the back of the cabin, but the place did have a patio with a table, a couple of chairs and a barbecue pit.

Duke pulled the sleeve of his jacket over his hand and pushed open the back door. She didn't notice any broken glass or splintered wood, so he must've picked the lock. The less she knew, the better.

She stepped through the door into a small room off the kitchen with a compact washer and dryer in the corner. Her breath coming in short spurts, she edged into the kitchen as Duke closed the door.

She hesitated at the entrance to the living room where a large stone fireplace took up half the wall.

"Maybe they don't get many renters here because it's not completely furnished or ready." Duke hovered at her shoulder. "Do you want to have a look?"

Beth had to peel her tongue from the roof of her mouth to talk. "I…I'm scared. This room… There's something evil here. Do you feel it?"

Duke stepped around her into the dark living room

and ran a hand along the mantel of the fireplace. "It's eerie, but I might be getting that vibe from you."

Beth took one shaky step after him. Curling her fingers around the gold locket at her throat, she closed her eyes. She could use some of Scarlett's magical tea about now.

She shuffled farther into the room, as if being drawn forward by some guiding force.

"Beth?"

Duke's voice seemed far away. Beth battled to get through the fear and revulsion to make her way toward a softer, more benevolent place at the end of this tunnel. The greenery of the Washington peninsula that had always caused her such anxiety rushed past her in a whirlwind. The blood-drenched terror that she'd faced in her shared vision with Scarlett swirled around her, but she kept her focus. There was something more, something sweet and precious, and she had to stay this course to get to it.

"Beth? Beth?"

The wood floor creaked beneath her and she fell to her knees. "I'm here. I'm back. I'll help you."

"Beth, my God."

Duke crouched beside her, his arm circling her waist. "Beth, are you okay? What's wrong with you?"

Twisting around to face him, she grabbed his jacket. "It's here, Duke. There's something here. Something led me here."

He stroked her hair. "I know, babe—the hypnosis, the visions, the red door and the birds have all led you here, but it's not enough. Even if we find out who owns the cabin, it might not be enough."

She pounded the floor through the Native American rug that covered it. "No, I mean it's here. There's something right here."

He dropped his gaze to the floor and ran his hand along the blanket, his brows creating a V between his eyes.

Just like that, he believed her.

"I don't see anything, Beth. It's just a rug." He flipped up one corner of the rug, exposing the original wood floor of the cabin, scarred and scratched. He pressed his hands against the slats of wood and one rocked beneath his hands.

"It's loose." His eyes flew to her face.

She breathed out the words. "It's here. I heard the wood creak beneath my feet. There's something here, Duke."

He reached into his pocket for his knife and flipped it open. He jimmied it between the loose slat and its neighbor. It lifted a half an inch.

"There's a cavity here."

Beth grabbed the knife, but Duke put his hand over hers. "Easy. We don't want anyone to know we've been here."

He took over and worked the blade back and forth until the wood came up from the floor. When he could get under the slat, he angled the knife and pumped it higher.

He eased up the slat and removed it. "Hand me your phone."

She knew what he wanted, and she turned her phone's light on before dropping it into his hand.

He aimed it into the space beneath the floor. "There's

a box in there. Looks like a small fisherman's tackle box. It's too big to fit through this opening. I'm going to have to remove a couple more pieces of flooring."

While Beth held the phone, Duke worked on two more slats until the opening was wide enough to accommodate the box.

"You do the honors."

With trembling hands, Beth reached into the cavity and pulled out the tin box. She didn't know what she expected—her real birth certificate? Adoption papers? A letter from her bio parents?

When she flung open the lid, she gasped and fell back on her heels. Whatever she'd expected to find, it didn't include this.

Duke grabbed a handful of the photos in the box and held them to the light. "What the hell? Nudie pictures?"

Beth studied the pictures fanned out in Duke's hand and gasped.

As she opened her mouth, an explosion rocked the cabin.

Chapter Sixteen

Duke's ears were ringing with the sound of the explosion. He reached for Beth, whose mouth was hanging open in shock. "Are you okay?"

She managed a nod.

His nostrils flared as he sniffed the air. A window in the front had shattered, but the cabin was intact, and he couldn't smell fire.

"The cabin's fine. The explosion came from outside."

He gathered all the photos from the box and shoved them into the camera case. "We need to get out of here."

Beth reached for the wood slats and slid the first one into place. They put the floor back the way it was and Beth covered it with the rug.

Duke slung the camera case across his body and hoisted Beth to her feet.

With the crutch snug beneath her arm, Beth moved as fast as she could for the kitchen.

Once outside, Duke could see black smoke rising from the front of the cabin. He turned and shut the door, clicking the lock back into place with his knife.

"Let's get in the car and call 9-1-1 when we can. We were just driving by when we heard an explosion, right?"

She licked her lips. "Got it."

They got to the front of the cabin and started down the path to the road when Beth gasped. "It's a tire."

With a sinking feeling in the pit of his stomach, Duke pushed through the gate to the road, stepping over twisted metal.

He swore when he saw the shell of his rented SUV twisted, blackened and still on fire.

Beth tried her phone. "Still no reception. I suppose we're going to have to admit to being out here unless you can think of a way to move that burning hulk and all its pieces somewhere else."

"We were walking up to the cabin to do research for your show and heard the explosion."

"We're going to have a chance to try out that story real soon." She cocked her head. "Sirens."

"Doug must've called it in."

She hooked her fingers in his back pocket. "What do you think happened to your car, other than the obvious?"

"Since dynamiting a rental car seems too suspect, even for Sheriff Musgrove, my guess is that it was an expertly placed shot to the gas tank."

"Easily explained away by an errant bullet or teenage prank."

"Or another rogue hunter, but now that Scarlett Easton has left town, who's the target this time?"

"Someone knew we were here, Duke." She rested her forehead against his back. "Someone didn't want us to find those pictures."

"That's going a little far to protect a few naked photos, don't you think. As far as I could tell, they were all grown women."

"It's more than that."

A fire truck roared down the access road, followed by a squad car and an ambulance.

"Hold that thought, Beth. We have some explaining to do."

OVER TWO HOURS LATER, after being dropped off by a deputy, they collapsed in Beth's hotel room.

Duke downed half a bottle of water in one gulp. "That went smoother than I expected. We were the victims, so the deputies didn't seem to care what we were doing at the cabin."

"At least they think it was a threat directed at me this time and not related to Scarlett's feud with the hunters."

"Yeah, but their solution was to tell you to leave town."

"It wasn't too long ago that your solution was the same."

He ran a hand down her back. "Because I wanted to protect you, not because I didn't want to deal with solving a crime. Sheriff Musgrove is a piece of work."

"At least the explosion got him off the golf course."

"You realize it's going to take about two minutes before the entire town of Timberline knows we were at that cabin."

"Who cares?" She patted the camera case. "We found the stash of pictures."

"I'm not sure what good they're going to do us unless you want to start a girlie magazine."

"That's because you didn't look at the pictures." She opened the camera case. "I did."

His pulse ticked up. "Something incriminating."

"Not exactly, but something very, very interesting." She pulled a handful of the pictures from the case and dropped them on the credenza, fanning them out. "Look at this picture and tell me what you think."

"First time I've ever had a woman ask me to look at provocative photos." He picked up the photo of a woman posing in the nude, tame by today's standards, and studied it. He dropped the picture as if it burned his fingers. "That looks like you."

"Exactly, and I can assure you I've never posed nude for anyone here in Timberline before."

He let that pass and picked up the picture again by the corner. He squinted at the pretty woman in the photo with the strawberry blond hair. Then he swallowed hard.

"Beth?"

She looked up from thumbing through the other photos. "Uh-huh?"

"Did you notice what this woman has around her neck?"

"No. An explosion interrupted my examination of the pictures."

He waved the photo in front of her face. "It looks like a necklace of some kind. I can't make out whether or not it's a locket, but I'm hazarding a guess it is."

Gasping, she snatched the photo from his hand. "You're right. A woman with strawberry blond hair wearing a necklace like mine."

Her bottom lip wobbled. "D-do you think this could be my mother?"

Duke plucked the photo from her hand and placed his thumb beneath the subject's chin, studying her face. He couldn't tell the color of her eyes, but the catlike shape matched Beth's, along with her wide cheekbones.

"You could be related, no doubt." Feeling like a voyeur, he turned the picture over. "What does it mean? Someone took risqué pictures of your mother and other women and then hid them under the floorboards of that cabin."

Beth lunged for her phone. "We need to find out who owns that cabin. All the deputy knew was that Raney Realty had the rental listing."

Beth tapped in Rebecca's number and left a message. "She's probably still busy with her open house."

Duke threw himself across the bed and rubbed his eyes. "I'm exhausted."

Beth stretched out beside him, propping up her head with her hand. "The strangest thing happened to me in that cabin. I felt like I was channeling Scarlett. Maybe some of her sensitivity rubbed off on me."

Duke's phone buzzed in his pocket and he pulled it out. "Mickey's calling. Hey, Mickey, this is my day off."

"How'd your meeting with the DEA go the other day? You never got back to me."

Duke's head rolled to the side and he watched Beth's eyelashes flutter closed. Had that meeting been before Beth's foot got caught in a bear trap or after someone had taken a shot at her?

"They're pulling all the files for me regarding drug activity in the area at the time of the kidnappings. Is someone getting anxious?"

"I'll tell you who's getting anxious—Stanley Gerber, that's who."

"Stan the man? The director of our division?"

"We had a situation, top secret. It all worked out, but Gerber wanted to know why you weren't on the case."

"And you told him I was in cold-case Siberia?"

"I did, and he wanted to know on whose orders."

"I guess Vasquez, his second in command, doesn't keep him up to date."

"I'm guessing he's having a few words with Vasquez right about now."

"Do you think he's going to pull me off the Timberline Trio case?"

Beth opened her eyes and nudged him with the heel of her hand.

"Maybe, but I'd like you to follow up with the drug connection first so we can show something for our efforts there."

"I'll see what I can do as soon as those files come through from the DEA." Duke sat up and swung his legs over the side of the bed. "What, no homework duty tonight?"

"It's Saturday. I've been coaching soccer all day."

"Father of the year, Mickey."

"I'm glad someone thinks so. Keep me posted on the drug angle and I'll put in a few hundred good words for you with Gerber."

When he ended the call Beth shot up next to him. "Are you getting yanked off this case?"

"Maybe, but not before I wrap up some loose ends."

She tapped her chest. "I'm your loose end. We need to discover what these pictures mean."

"Let's get some dinner while you wait for Rebecca's callback."

"I can't face going into town tonight. After hearing about that explosion, the townspeople just might come after me with pitchforks."

"There's that new development near Evergreen with a couple of chain restaurants."

"I could use a bland chain restaurant about now, but I need a shower after crawling around that cabin floor."

"Meet you back here in thirty minutes?"

"I think I can manage that."

He went back to his own room, his mind in turmoil. He and Beth had figured someone had to have been tracking them to know their whereabouts this afternoon—unless Rebecca had told someone.

If someone had put a tracking device on his rental car, he'd never know now that the car had been destroyed. The rental company had already towed it away.

Why wouldn't someone want them to find some old pictures? Unless that cabin had something to do with the Timberline Trio case, these threats against Beth made no sense at all.

He'd been concerned when she'd decided to stay in town because he'd figured the people threatening her would assume she was still on the Timberline Trio case, but maybe the attacks had nothing to do with the Timberline Trio.

Maybe someone had objected to Beth's personal quest all along. But why? Why should one woman's journey to find her beginnings cause anyone to feel uneasy?

Showered and changed, Duke returned to Beth's room. She opened the door, her face alight with excitement. "Rebecca called me back and she's going to look into that property as soon as she gets the chance. She's having dinner with her fiancé, but he's flying back to New York later and she's going to return to her office for some work."

"Then let's enjoy our dinner with some endless breadsticks and all-you-can-eat salad."

She paced in front of him. "I don't think I even need my crutches anymore."

They drove across town in Beth's rental to the newer area that owed its existence to Evergreen Software. When they walked into the restaurant, they barely warranted a glance from anyone.

These were the newer residents of Timberline and, except for that glitch with Wyatt Carson, they were far removed from the Timberline Trio tragedy.

Over dinner, Duke ran his new theory past Beth. "I was thinking in the shower."

"That's where I do all my best thinking." She bit off the end of a breadstick and grinned. That interlude in the cabin had transformed Beth from the scared creature of this afternoon. He'd expected her to be wrung dry from the experience and the discovery, but she'd been energized by it—vindicated.

"Beth, it occurred to me that the threats against you may not have anything to do with the Timberline Trio case. It could be that someone here doesn't want you to discover your identity. Maybe someone discovered your true purpose and has been doing everything he can to drive you away from that purpose."

She stabbed a tomato with her fork. "I thought of

that, too. What if...? What if my birth parents don't want me?"

He dropped his fork and interlaced his fingers with hers. "Are you prepared for that?"

"I came out here to find the truth. I can handle it."

"Beth." He squeezed her fingers. "You came out here because you thought you were Heather Brice and you expected to be reunited with your long-lost, loving family. It's not going to be that way."

"I know." She gave him a misty smile. "But the fact that you stayed with me, helped me, didn't turn away from me when I told you about the miscarriage...well, that means more to me than ten loving families."

He brought her fingers to his lips and kissed the tips. "I'll ride this out with you until the end."

After dinner, they closed the place down over a shared dessert and coffee for him, decaf tea for her.

As they got in the car, Beth's phone rang.

"Hi, Rebecca. I'm with Duke. I'm putting you on speakerphone. Do you have anything for us?"

"I have the owner of that cabin for you. You know Serena Hopewell, the bartender at Sutter's?"

"Serena owns the cabin?"

"She's owned it for over twenty years."

"Does she live there?"

"Doesn't look like she ever lived there. It's been a rental, under Raney Realty, for quite some time."

Duke leaned toward Beth's phone. "Inherited property?"

"I don't think so."

"Who'd she buy it from?"

"Some management company—LRS Corp. Never heard of it. Hey!"

"What's wrong?"

"My lights just flickered."

Duke grabbed the phone from Beth. "Rebecca, are you in the office alone?"

"Of course I am. Who else would be nutty enough to be working on Saturday night?" She cursed. "The lights just went out in my office completely. Is it raining?"

Duke and Beth exchanged a glance and Beth asked, "Are your doors locked?"

"Of course. What's wrong with you two?"

"Rebecca." Duke kept his tone calm. "Your life is in danger."

As he uttered his last syllable, the line went dead.

"Rebecca? Rebecca?"

He tossed his phone to Beth as he tried Rebecca's number. "Call 9-1-1."

Rebecca's phone rang until it rolled over to voice mail.

Beth jerked her head toward Duke and covered the phone. "The operator is asking me what the emergency is. What should I say?"

He snapped his fingers and she handed the phone to him. "A woman I was speaking to on the phone thought she had an intruder and then her phone went dead. I can't reach her now."

"Name and address?"

"Rebecca Geist with Peninsula Realty." He gave the operator the address of Rebecca's office and his name, and then he ended the call. "A deputy's on the way, but so are we."

Beth had retrieved her phone from the console and had been trying Rebecca's number.

"Any luck?"

"Keeps going straight to voice mail." Beth hugged herself, bunching her hands against her arms. "I'm worried. Someone must've known she was doing all this research for us. We should've warned her against going back to her office alone."

"She was going back to do some work, not just for us. Anyone who knows Rebecca must know she burns the midnight oil at the office."

"Especially someone like Bill Raney."

As he hit the accelerator, Duke drummed his thumbs on the steering wheel. "She said some corporation had sold the property to Serena. Do you remember the name?"

"It was three letters. L something, but I'm not sure."

"Why harm Rebecca over information like that? She's not the only one who has access to those records. That's public information."

"I hope that's you thinking out loud because I have no idea."

"Unless it's just to further intimidate you, drive you away."

"Yeah, like that's going to happen."

"Beth—" he put a hand on her bouncing knee "—we can research that corporation and Bill Raney and Serena Hopewell from any place. Maybe you should spread it around that you're leaving, there's no story and you're tired of the pranks against you."

"And then actually leave?"

"Yes, leave. We can continue looking into all of it— the identities of those women, the history of that cabin."

"I'll think about it." She pointed out the window. "Look! It's a squad car in front of Rebecca's office."

"Good."

As he pulled in behind the police vehicle, an ambulance came up the road, sirens wailing.

"Duke." Beth grabbed his arm.

He threw the car into Park and shot out of the driver's side just as another squad car squealed to a stop.

His gut knotted as he charged up to the front of the building.

Deputy Stevens stepped in front of him. "Oh, it's you. You called it in, right?"

"What happened? Where's Rebecca Geist?"

Stevens gestured him inside and Beth grabbed the back of his jacket, limping behind him.

Holding up a hand, Stevens said, "Beth, you might not want to go in there."

"The hell I won't."

The revolving lights of the emergency vehicles lit up a hellish scene inside the offices of Peninsula Realty. Papers littered the floor, file cabinets lay on their sides, spilling their guts, computer equipment had been smashed and in the center of it all, Rebecca Geist broken and bloodied.

Chapter Seventeen

Beth cried out and staggered toward Rebecca. She dropped to the floor beside her. "She's still breathing. She's still alive."

"We know that, Beth. The EMTs are here—make way."

Duke touched her shoulder. "Let them do their work, Beth."

She covered her face with her arm as Duke helped her to her feet. "Oh, my God. It looks bad."

"She took a bad beating, but maybe we saved her life. There's nothing we can do for her now." Duke led Beth outside, where they spoke to the deputies.

They explained how Rebecca had been doing research for them on some cabins and how she'd complained of the office lights going out while she was on the phone with them.

Stevens asked, "Did she say anything else after that?"

"Her phone went dead and that's when we called 9-1-1."

"I was the one who responded first and I think I scared the guy off."

"Did he leave any footprints? A weapon? If he beat her with his fists, you're going to be looking for someone with some battered hands."

"I think he may have used a hole-punch."

"A hole-punch?"

"You know. One of those heavy, three-hole punchers? There was one next to the body. I'm sorry—next to Rebecca." Stevens wiped his brow beneath his hat despite the chill in the damp air. "She was conscious when I got here and her pulse was strong. I think she has a good chance of making it."

"Her fiancé." Beth folded her hands across her stomach. "She'd just had dinner with him and he was on his way to New York."

"Her coworkers will know how to reach him. From what I understand, he's loaded, flies a private jet into Timberline." Stevens waved the other deputy into the office. "What kind of research was she doing for you? Was it for the show?"

"There's not going to be any show on the Timberline Trio for *Cold Case Chronicles.*" Duke curled his arm around her hip and pinched her. "Rebecca didn't come up with anything new, and Beth's decided there's not enough for a whole episode on the case."

"I'm sure quite a few people will be relieved to hear that. It's a little different when you have the FBI working on something behind the scenes and not splashing it all over TV."

"I may be wrapping up here soon, too."

"Well, maybe those kids were snatched by that Quileute creature."

"Not even the Quileute believe that, Sheriff." Beth's lips formed a thin line.

They said good-night to the sheriff and Duke caught Stevens's arm. "You'll let us know how it goes with Rebecca, right?"

Stevens shot a sidelong glance at Musgrove shouting orders and nodded. "I'll let you know as soon as I hear anything."

Beth collapsed in the passenger seat. "I hope she's going to make it."

"I hope so, too. She had a lot of head wounds and those bleed profusely. It might look worse than it is."

She pushed her hair from her face and pinned her shoulders against the seat back. "Before I do leave, Duke, I'm going to talk to Serena about her cabin."

"Are you going to ask her who sold it to her? Because I can't remember what Rebecca told us."

"That's one question."

"You might want to ask her how she could afford to buy a cabin like that on a waitress's salary—be more discreet than that, but you know what I mean. Don't you think that's weird?"

"That and the fact that she doesn't even live in it and Doug told us it's not rented out much."

"Be careful, Beth. Let people know you're done with the story, that you're leaving town."

"I will. I don't want to get anyone else involved. I've put Scarlett in danger and now Rebecca."

"And maybe Gary Binder."

"Do you think he knew something about that cabin? Do you think he was at the hotel to talk to me?"

"Maybe, or it could be his drug connection." He

tapped his phone. "I got an automated email from the DEA tonight indicating the files I requested are ready for viewing, so I'm going to work on that tomorrow. And you're going to work on getting a flight out of Seattle. I can drive you to Sea-Tac anytime."

That night they made love again and she held on to Duke for dear life. If she had to give up her search in Timberline, he might be the only family she ever had.

THE NEXT MORNING DUKE, already dressed in running clothes, woke her up with a kiss. "Wish you could come with me."

She held up her foot. "As soon as this heals, I'll be right there with you."

"Do you want to have brunch at that River Café when I get back?"

"Okay, and then I'm going to find Serena and that'll be it for me."

"Which means you'll be on your laptop this morning looking into flights from Seattle to LA and on the phone with Scott to tell him the story's off."

"Yes, sir." She saluted. "Scott's going to be so happy this fell through. He warned his father it was a bad story."

"So, you get to keep your life and pump up Scott's ego in the process. It's a win-win."

Two hours later they parted ways after brunch. Duke's rental-car agency had replaced his SUV. Luckily for them, they had used different rental companies or one company would be left wondering just what the hell was going on in Timberline.

That was exactly what she wanted to know.

She drove into town, wishing she hadn't eaten so much at brunch. When she sat down at the bar at Sutter's she didn't want Serena to think she was there just for her.

A call to Chloe had already confirmed that Serena was working today. When didn't she work the bar at Sutter's? Maybe that was how she could afford the up-keep on that cabin.

All eyes seem riveted to her when she walked into the restaurant. If someone wanted her out of Timber-line, it could be any one of these people.

She hobbled to the bar on one crutch and hopped up on a stool.

Serena placed a cocktail napkin in front of her. "What can I get you?"

"I'm just going to have lunch again, if that's okay."

"Fine with me." Serena dropped a menu on the bar and got a beer for another customer.

Beth made a show of studying the menu and then closed it and folded her hands on top of it.

Serena returned. "Ready?"

"I'll have a ginger ale and a bowl of lentil soup."

Serena shot the ginger ale into a glass from a noz-zle. "Not too popular around here anymore, are you?"

"No, and I can't do a show when the residents have turned against me. I'm calling it quits on this story."

"You can't blame people for getting cold feet. A lot of weird stuff has gone down since you've been here."

"Yeah, like someone shooting the gas tank of Agent Harper's rental car and blowing it up."

"Shows how desperate some of these people are. You don't mess with the FBI."

"That explosion—" Beth toyed with her straw "—happened outside of your cabin."

Serena's eyes narrowed.

"I mean, you own that cabin, right?"

"I do. Excuse me." Serena moved to the other end of the bar to take an order. She didn't return to Beth until she brought the soup.

"One lentil soup."

"Did you inherit that cabin?"

"Who, me? My folks never had any money, didn't even come from this area."

"So, you bought it?"

"I bought it after the Timberline kidnappings. Prices dropped off then. The lumber company had already pulled up roots. I got a good deal from an anxious seller."

"That person must've regretted it once Evergreen Software moved in here and prices went up again."

"Actually, it wasn't a person, just some big corporation that owned other properties. I got lucky."

"Is the corporation still around? What was the name of it?"

"Why do you care?"

Damn, she'd come across as too nosy. She took out her phone and feigned interest in her text messages. "I don't, really. Just curious—occupational hazard."

"I don't remember the name of the company. I'd have to look it up in my paperwork, wherever that stuff is now. Oh, hello, Jordan. Can I get you something?"

Smiling at Beth, he pointed to her soup. "I'll have some of that and a cup of coffee, if you've got some fresh."

"Coming right up."

Jordan swiveled on his stool to face her. "I heard you're not going to do the story."

"Word travels fast." She placed her phone on the bar.

"Small town." He lifted a shoulder. "Too bad."

"Are you one of those who was pro-story? I would've thought you'd be against it because of the business interests you have here."

"Thanks, sweetheart." He dumped some cream into the coffee Serena had brought him. "I'm a forward-thinking person. I think any publicity is good publicity. That whole mess with Carson kidnapping those kids and playing the hero didn't hurt business or our reputation. Some people are too sensitive."

"Like your friend Bill Raney."

"Bill has a lot to be sensitive about. He's a failure. People like me and that little firecracker, Rebecca Geist... we have nothing to fear."

"Did you hear what happened to Rebecca last night?"

"Damned shame, but then, you tend to attract unwanted attention when you're successful. Like you." He sipped his coffee and met her gaze over the rim. "Do you really want to give up?"

"I don't consider it giving up. There's just not enough here to produce a compelling story."

He winked. "You haven't talked to me yet."

"That's not from a lack of effort. You're a busy man, Mr. Young."

"Jordan, and I've got some time right now. Maybe what I have to show you will make you reconsider your decision."

Her heart thumped. Jordan had been around for a

while. He just might know more of Timberline's secrets than anyone else since he also seemed to be tight with the town's movers and shakers.

"That depends on what you've got for me."

"You know that cabin you wanted to see out on Raven Road? The one where the agent's car exploded?" He hunched forward and cupped a hand around his mouth. "I can get you inside."

Beth's gaze darted to Serena counting money at the register. "It belongs to Serena."

"Yes and no. Let's just say it's more complicated than that."

"How can you get into the cabin?" She couldn't exactly admit to Jordan that she'd already been inside. She didn't want to get Duke into any trouble, especially if it turned out that Jordan knew the real owner.

"Let's just say I'm like this—" he crossed his fingers "—with the management company."

"H…he doesn't have to be there, does he?"

"He doesn't even have to know. It'll be our secret." He put his finger over his lips and glanced at Serena.

"Okay. What time?"

"How about right now? I don't have any meetings until later this afternoon." He rubbed his hands together when Serena put his soup in front of him. "Thanks."

When she walked away, he dropped his spoon. "I'll tell you what. You're staying at one of my hotels, the Timberline, right?"

"Yeah, the one that needs cameras."

"I have a little business to attend to there. Why don't you head back to the hotel, let me finish my lunch, and I'll meet you there and we can go over to the Ravens together."

"The Ravens?"

"That's what the cabin's called. Most of the owners of these cabins, especially the ones outside of town, named their places."

"I didn't even know that road was called Raven Road." Beth's hands grew clammy just thinking about the Ravens and she grabbed a napkin and crumpled it in her fist. Her breath started coming in shallow gusts, and she slid from the stool. "Can you excuse me for a minute?"

She made a beeline for the ladies' room and hunched over the sink, breathing in and out. Just talking about the cabin was causing her to freak out. How would she handle another visit there? But Jordan was offering her another opportunity to take a look at the place and she couldn't refuse.

She splashed water on her face and gave herself a pep talk in the mirror. Pasting a smile on her face, she returned to the bar.

"Sorry about that. So, the Ravens is on Raven Road."

Jordan studied her face for a second. "It's a local name, not on the maps. Ravens are important to Quileute legends, so I guess that's where it came from. Does that sound like a plan? You can wait for me in the parking lot of the hotel. I won't be long, and then you can decide if you really want to give up on this story."

"Okay. I'd love to see inside that cabin…for my own reasons."

"Excellent." He took a spoonful of soup into his mouth.

"Anything else?" Serena picked up Beth's bowl and dropped the check.

"No, thanks." Beth left some cash on the bar, swept her phone into her palm and nodded to Jordan.

Beth took her time getting back to the hotel, since Jordan had to finish his lunch anyway. She stopped by the market and picked up some water and a bottle of wine. If this was going to be her last night in Timberline with Duke, she might as well make it special.

She pulled her phone out of her pocket to leave him a text message. She tapped her screen, but her phone wouldn't wake up. She powered it down and tried again. The battery must've died.

Jordan had said he had meetings in the afternoon, so they'd be done at the Ravens before Duke finished working on the DEA files anyway.

When she pulled into the hotel's parking lot, Jordan was just walking out of the hotel.

She grabbed her crutch and scrambled from the car. "That was fast."

"It was just soup. What took you so long?"

She held up the plastic bag with one hand. "Stopped for a few things."

"Perishable?"

"No."

"Why don't you leave them in your car?" He looked at his watch. "My meeting was earlier than I thought, and I'm going to have to make this fast."

"Oh, okay." Leaning back into the car, Beth placed the bag on the passenger seat.

She used her crutch to navigate to his black sedan and the open passenger door.

"How's that foot of yours?"

"It's getting better. In a few days I think I can put more pressure on it and get around without using a crutch."

He helped her into the car and slammed the door.

On the way to the cabin he asked about her theories of the kidnappings.

She stared out the window at the passing scenery before answering. She really hadn't given the Timberline Trio much thought, especially once she'd found out she wasn't one of them.

"I'm not sure, maybe child trafficking, as awful as that sounds. Maybe those kids were just in the wrong place at the wrong time."

"It was a strange and scary time, especially for those with children."

"You didn't have children to worry about?"

"My wife and I were never fortunate in that regard."

"And then you lost your wife… I'm sorry. People do talk in a small town."

"Lorna drowned."

"I'm so sorry."

She'd changed the mood in the car by mentioning his wife. He seemed thoughtful as he gazed over the steering wheel.

He never remarried, so Lorna must've been the love of his life.

When he made the turn onto Raven Road, her fingers curled into the leather on either side of the seat and her pulse rate quickened. She'd thought getting into the cabin and finding the picture of the woman with the locket had dispelled her fears, but the anxiety still hovered at the edges of her mind.

Jordan dragged a hand across his face. "Did you call Agent Harper? I know he was interested in the cabin, too."

"My phone's battery died. He's working, anyway."

"On a Sunday?"

"He works when he gets the call."

"I have to admit I'm a little relieved."

She tilted her head. "Why is that?"

"He's an officer of the law and, technically, I'm entering the cabin without the owner's knowledge."

She smirked. If Jordan only knew Duke had been breaking and entering just yesterday. "I don't think he'd report you. So, do you think the Ravens is connected to the Timberline Trio kidnappings?"

"Could be. Back in the day, it was used for some illicit activities."

"Really?" Like prostitution? Her stomach felt sick at the thought of the pretty strawberry blonde involved in anything sordid.

"I don't know that much about it, but the Ravens had a reputation around that time. I thought that's why you were out here yesterday."

"I think Duke, Agent Harper, may have gotten some hint about something like that, but we barely got to the front door when the car exploded."

"Makes you wonder if some of those old characters are still hanging around, like what happened to Binder. Coincidental that he died in a hit-and-run accident right after telling the FBI a little about Timberline's drug culture."

A chill swept across Beth's body and she hunched her shoulders. She dug her phone out of her pocket and tried waking it up again.

"Still dead?"

"Yeah." She dropped it back in her pocket.

"Reception is bad out this way, anyway."

He swung around the yellow tape tied to a tree where Duke's car had been parked and rolled up the pathway to the cabin.

"Stay right there, Beth. I'll help you out."

He appeared at the passenger door and jingled a set of keys as he gave her his arm for support. "We can get inside the right way this time."

"This time?"

"Well, you didn't get in at all yesterday, did you?"

"N…no."

Her uneasiness still nibbled at the edges of her brain, but it differed from the sheer terror she felt yesterday.

He held her arm as they walked up the two steps to the front door. He used the key to unlock two locks on the door and pushed it open.

The front door opened right onto the sitting room where she and Duke had removed the floorboards and found the pictures.

"After you."

She hesitated, and Jordan put a hand on the small of her back. "We're not going to get caught."

As soon as Beth entered the room, beads of sweat broke out on her forehead. Her dry mouth made it hard to swallow. The room closed around her and she hung on to her crutch as the room began to spin.

"You feel it, don't you, Beth? She led you here, didn't she? Your mother led you to the place where she was murdered."

Chapter Eighteen

Duke pushed back from the desk in the conference room at the sheriff's station and stretched. If the Bureau pulled him off this case, at least he could leave with a good report regarding the drug trade in Timberline and who was behind it. A biker gang called the Lords of Chaos controlled the drug trade on the peninsula. They also ran women and weapons. A thorough investigation of that gang might lead to additional information about the kidnappings.

He checked his phone. Nothing from Beth. He texted her, but the message didn't show as Delivered. He tried calling and his call went straight to voice mail.

Maybe she was getting something from Serena.

Unger tapped on the open door. "Thought you'd want to know. Rebecca Geist is out of surgery. It looks like she's going to pull through, but they're keeping her in an induced coma until the swelling on her brain goes down."

"Thank God. Did her fiancé make it out here?"

"He's on a flight back right now. Do you need anything in here?"

"No. I skipped lunch, so I might take a break in a few minutes and pick up something."

"I can recommend the sandwich place two doors down."

"Thanks." When Unger left, Duke rubbed his eyes and went back to the Lords of Chaos and their dirty deeds.

As he scanned a bulleted list, a name jumped out at him—LRS Corporation. That was the name Rebecca had mentioned before she'd been attacked. He ran his finger beneath the text on the screen. The Lords of Chaos had rented several properties from LRS and used some of them for their illegal activities, including cooking meth.

Duke switched to a search engine and entered *LRS Corporation, Timberline, Washington*. He skimmed through the relevant hits.

LRS stood for and was owned by Lawrence Richard Strathmore, who'd passed away about twenty years ago. He'd been around during the time of the kidnappings.

He clicked through a couple of biographies. The man and the corporation had owned a lot of property in Timberline at one time. His wife had passed before he did and they had one daughter.

Duke whistled through his teeth. Strathmore's daughter, Lorna, had married Jordan Young.

Duke jumped up from his chair and stuck his head out the door. "Unger?"

"Yeah?"

"Need to ask you a few questions."

Unger walked around the corner with a sandwich in his hand. "Sorry, man. I would've gotten you something when I went over there earlier if I'd known you were gonna be holed up in here all morning."

"That's okay." Duke waved him to the chair as he perched on the edge of the conference table. "Jordan Young is a widower, right?"

"Yeah, his wife died about ten years ago—drowned."

"His wife was Lorna? Lorna Strathmore?"

"Not sure about her maiden name, but Lorna's right."

"Wasn't she loaded?"

"I heard something like that. Young got his money the old-fashioned way—he married it."

"You ever heard of LRS Corporation?"

"I've seen the name on a few things. Why?"

"That was the name of Young's father-in-law's company—owned a lot of property in Timberline."

"Now Young owns a lot of property in Timberline. Why are you asking?"

"Just a curious connection between him and something Beth was looking into." Duke rubbed his chin. "You know much about him?"

"Between me and you?" Duke poked his head out the door and then closed it. "He likes the ladies, and I think he shares that with my boss."

"Is the sheriff married? I don't see a problem for Young since he's widowed."

"I guess I'm being too discreet for the big-city boy, huh? What I mean is Young is into hookers, and I think Sheriff Musgrove is, too, which is a problem for both of them, as far as I can tell."

"Wow, you need to get rid of that guy. He's going to bring the department a world of hurt otherwise."

"Tell me about it." He swung open the door. "Anyway, that's about all I know about Young, about all I want to know about him."

"Thanks, Unger."

Duke tapped his thumbs on the edge of his keyboard. Jordan Young sold that cabin to Serena Hopewell. Why? Was he the one who'd stashed those pictures under the floorboards? Were those women hookers? Was the one who had Beth's locket a hooker?

He needed to reach Beth, tell her everything. He tried her phone again, and again it went to voice mail. This time he left her a detailed message about Jordan Young.

Had she even seen Serena today? Maybe Serena had already given Beth the same info about Young.

He shut down the computer and stacked his files. Then he locked the conference room door behind him.

"Unger, I'm going to Sutter's for some lunch."

"All right, but the sandwiches down the street are just as good."

"I need something else at Sutter's."

The Evergreen lunch hour must've ended because Duke walked into a mostly empty restaurant. He noted Serena working behind the bar and wove his way through the dining room tables to get there.

"You just missed your girlfriend, the TV reporter."

"Did she talk to you about the cabin?" Duke hunched forward on the bar.

Serena's eyes widened. "Why are you two so interested in my cabin? It's just a cabin like any other on the outskirts of town, and it has no relation to the Timberline Trio case."

"That you know of."

"Do you want something to drink or are you just here to harass me?"

"Who sold you that cabin, Serena?"

"Oh, for God's sake. I don't remember—some corporation."

"Why are you lying? The LRS Corporation sold you that cabin—LRS, as in Lawrence Richard Strathmore, as in Jordan Young's father-in-law. Only, Young had control of the corporation when he sold the cabin to you. Why'd he sell it to you? Why'd he give you such a sweet deal?"

Serena backed up to the register, her arms across her chest. "What do you want from me?"

"Let's start with the truth. What was Young using that cabin for and why'd he want to get rid of it?"

He lunged over the bar and grabbed her arm. "And what's this tattoo on your wrist? Does that *LC* stand for the Lords of Chaos?"

She jerked away from him. "You want answers? Talk to Jordan Young."

"Is there a problem?" A restaurant employee wearing a shirt and tie approached them with his phone out. "Do I need to call the police?"

Duke released Serena and pulled out his badge. "I just have a few questions for Ms. Hopewell."

"It's all right, Randy." Serena flicked her fingers.

When the manager walked away, Duke asked, "Where can I find Young?"

"I'm not sure." Serena rubbed the tattoo on her wrist. "But he was in here the same time your friend was here when she was asking me questions about the cabin, sat right next to her. Maybe even did something to her phone."

Duke's blood ran cold. "What?"

"She went to the ladies', left her phone on the bar, and it looked like Jordan picked it up."

"Did they leave together?" Duke's heart was thundering in his chest.

"No, but..."

"But what?" Duke's hands fisted on the bar. "I'm sure the FBI can find something on you, Serena, from your years running with the Lords of Chaos."

Her jaw hardened. "But she left and then he left not long after they were having a hushed conversation—like he didn't want me to hear what they were saying."

"And did you hear anything they were saying?"

"I heard him mention the Ravens."

"The Ravens? What's that?"

"That's the name of my cabin—you know, the one you broke into before someone blew up your car."

BETH DROPPED TO the nearest chair, her crutch falling to the ground. "My mother was murdered? Here?"

"I'm afraid so, Beth." Jordan pulled a gun from his pocket and aimed it at her.

"The picture." Beth put a hand to her temple where her pulse throbbed. "The woman with the strawberry blond hair... Was that her?"

"I knew you'd found those pictures. I knew you and Agent Harper were out here, and I thought I could stop you by shooting out the gas tank on his car, but I was too late." He smoothed the pad of his thumb over his eyebrow. "I knew she'd led you to those pictures. How else could you have found them?"

Beth folded her hands in her lap, trying to hold it all together even though she felt amazingly relaxed—maybe because she'd reached the moment of truth.

"You don't seem surprised or skeptical that a dead woman could've led someone to a bunch of pictures."

He sat on the arm of the chair across from her. "That's because your mother was Quileute and so are you."

Scarlett reaching out to her and bringing her along in her dream quest made sense now, but with that hair color, her mother probably wasn't full-blooded Quileute.

Beth trapped her hands between her knees. Jordan Young most likely murdered her mother for reasons she didn't know yet, but she wasn't ready to go there with him. He still might let her go.

"Why did you take me here? Why are you telling me all this?"

"You want to know your identity, don't you?" He spread his hands. "That's why you concocted the story that you were here for the Timberline Trio, although you thought you were Heather Brice for a while, didn't you? I would've been content if you had continued along that path. Why didn't you?"

"Duke—Agent Harper—requested DNA from the Brices and ran a cross-check with mine." She plucked her useless phone from her pocket. "I've called him, you know. I told him I was on my way here."

"That would be hard to do with a phone without a battery." He dipped into his front pocket and held up a battery pinched between his thumb and forefinger.

Beth's stomach rolled. "Are you going to tell me about my mother? Her name? Why she was murdered?"

"Your mother." He stroked his chin. "Angie was lovely, delicate, so much more refined than Lorna, even though my wife was the one with the money."

"Your wife died. You said she drowned." Beth clenched her bottom lip between her teeth to keep it from trembling. Had he killed his wife, too?

"That was later." He ran a hand through his salt-and-pepper hair. "When Angie got pregnant, I realized it was my wife's fault we couldn't have a baby."

The knots in Beth's gut tightened, almost cutting off her breath.

Jordan Young was her father.

His blue eyes, the precise shade of her own, lit up. "That's right, Beth. I'm your father."

She gripped the arms of the chair and vaulted out of it, but her legs wouldn't support her and she stumbled backward, falling onto the chair's cushion.

"Why? Why did you kill her? Because she got pregnant and had your child?"

His brows collided over his nose. "If she had gone away quietly, like she did at first, it wouldn't have been a problem. But she decided to come back. I was married to a very wealthy woman and had a father-in-law who thought the world of me. How do you think he would've felt after discovering I'd gotten some Indian pregnant?"

Beth flinched. "But I must've been two years old. She'd kept the secret that long."

"You weren't two at the time. Your adoptive parents changed your age and birth certificate to mask your true identity. You were a baby, barely one year old. Angie left when you were first born, but then she returned. She shouldn't have come back, Beth."

"You murdered my mother to keep her quiet? To get rid of a messy problem?"

"It was more of an accident, to tell you the truth. She knew I was never going to leave Lorna, and she knew I wanted her to keep quiet." He clucked his tongue. "Your mother wasn't as sweet and innocent as she appeared. You have the pictures to prove that. She tried to extort money out of me."

"Maybe she just wanted child support for me."

"Whatever you want to call it. She also found the pictures of the other women—silly bitch to think she was the only one."

Beth's nose stung. How could she be related to this monster? Duke had been right. It would've been better to stay in the dark.

"Did you shoot at me? Set the bear traps? Beat Rebecca?"

"Bill was more than happy to help with Rebecca. I was just trying to scare you away, but you wouldn't go away—just like your mother. As soon as I heard Beth St. Regis of *Cold Case Chronicles* was in town, I knew there was a problem."

"Y…you knew who I was all this time?"

"Of course. When I offered you up to the market, I insisted on having some say in where you went."

"So, I have you to thank for my cold, unfeeling parents."

He shrugged. "What do you expect from a couple who would take a child off the black market? But I was your father, Beth. I followed your career with great pride—until you came here."

A movement beyond Jordan's shoulder caught her eye. Something had flickered at the window of the back door.

"What led you here?" Jordan glanced at the fireplace. "Did she speak to you from beyond? I knew she had the gift, not as strong as Scarlett Easton's, but I always feared it."

Was that Duke at the back door? She coughed. "It started with the Pacific Chorus frog. It was a toy I'd had from my earliest years. I finally tracked it down to Timberline because of the Wyatt Carson story on TV. And it was the visions and nightmares I'd always had of a lush forest filled with terror."

A glimmer of light flashed from the laundry room for a second and Beth held her breath as Jordan cocked his head.

She rushed on. "Why would I feel such fear? Was I here in the cabin at one point?"

"You were here when I murdered her."

Beth bent over at the waist, bitter bile rising in her throat. "You killed her in front of her child?"

"It wasn't planned. It was an accident. She just wouldn't shut up about what I owed her and how she was going to get it out of me." He waved the gun in her face and for the first time she really believed he'd kill her.

"I'm not like my mother. I don't want anything out of you. I was going to leave Timberline anyway. I'll never come back here."

"We're alike, you and I." He wagged a finger at her.

"I could see that when I watched your show. A hard charger. I admire that, Beth."

"I am like you. I understand why you did what you did. You were only protecting your position."

"I murdered Lorna, too, you know."

Beth covered her ears. "I don't want to know what you did. I don't care."

"I saved you that day, Beth. As I stabbed your mother and rivers of blood soaked your body, I saved you."

Beth choked and covered her mouth.

"But I don't think I can save you this time. If you'd just stopped digging. If you hadn't gone to Scarlett. If you hadn't asked Rebecca for help. If you hadn't been part Quileute and your mother's daughter."

"Where is she? What did you do with my mother's body after you stabbed her to death?"

Jordan rose from the arm of the chair and placed his hand against the wall above the mantel. "I left her here."

Beth cried out and staggered to her feet. "You bastard!"

The gun dangled at his side and she lunged for it.

Jordan raised his arm, but she was close to him and bumped his forearm.

"Drop it, Young." Duke burst into the living room, his weapon trained on Jordan.

Jordan grabbed her around the waist, gripping the gun in the other hand.

A shot rang out and Beth screamed over the ringing in her ears.

Jordan slumped against her, his blood pumping out of the wound in his chest, covering her body.

She'd returned to where she began.

Epilogue

Safe in the crook of Duke's arm, Beth watched the demolition crew enter the Ravens, followed by a hazmat team from the FBI and Deputy Unger.

"You don't need to be here, Beth."

"I do. My mother led me back here and I owe it to her to witness her release."

He rubbed her back. "He didn't admit to anything involving Gary Binder, did he?"

"No, everything else was him and Bill Raney."

"The sheriff's department has already arrested Raney for assault and attempted murder. They're going to try to determine how much he knew about Young's activities."

"Serena, too?"

"She's left town."

"I guess there's your answer."

"Maybe, or she's protecting herself against questions about the biker gang, the Lords of Chaos, she used to run with."

"Rebecca's doing better. I visited her this morning. Her fiancé is going to take her to Hawaii on a sort of a convalescence-slash-vacation in a week."

"You talked to Scarlett?"

"She's still in San Francisco and is heading for New York after." Beth rested her head against Duke's shoulder. "She wasn't too surprised when she found out about my mother's heritage."

"She didn't know Angie?"

"Her grandmother had known my grandmother, but they didn't live on the reservation and Angie was a free spirit. When she came back to the rez twenty-five years ago, pregnant, she'd talked about a rich fiancé who was going to take her around the world."

"And she never left Timberline." Duke shook his head. "Did Jordan talk much about the black market he used to…place you?"

"No. Do you think it's related to the disappearance of the Timberline Trio?"

"I do, and I think they're both related to the Lords of Chaos. I was at least able to give the Bureau a thorough report of the gang's activities in this area."

"Where to next for you?"

"Wherever you are." He kissed the side of her head.

"I'm sure the FBI is going to have a thing or two to say about that."

"After I tag along with you to LA, I think I'm headed back to Chicago, but not before we make some serious plans."

"I like the sound of that." She fluffed his hair back from his face.

"Are you going to do a segment on finding your mother? It definitely qualifies as a cold case, and the ratings would be sky-high."

She tightened her hold on his arm as the door of the

cabin swung wide. "I don't care about the ratings, Duke. Some things are not for the public's consumption."

The hazmat crew navigated the porch steps, wheeling a gurney with a black bag on top of it.

Beth sucked in a breath and Duke pushed off the stone planter and helped Beth to her feet.

As the gurney made its way down the path, a surge of people, Quileute in their native ceremonial dress, gathered on either side of the procession.

A low chant rose and puffs of incense scented the air around them.

One of the elders approached Beth and bowed her head. "You have family now, Beth St. Regis, a whole nation behind you."

With tears in her eyes, Beth nodded and touched the old woman's silver hair.

When law enforcement, the emergency vehicles and the procession of Quileute had cleared out, Duke took her in his arms. "I'm sorry, Beth, for all of it."

"I'm glad I found out. Now I can get to know my mother for the person she was. All the doubts and fears are gone."

He stroked her hair. "It's time to rewrite the past for both of us now. I want to create what we both missed out on—a family. If that's just us or ten kids or one, it doesn't matter. Are you ready for that, Beth?"

She curled her arms around his waist and pressed her cheek against the steady beat of his heart. "I'm ready for all of it, and as long as you're by my side, I know I'm home. Duke Harper, you're the man of my dreams."

* * * * *

Carol Ericson's miniseries
TARGET: TIMBERLINE
continues next month with
ARMY RANGER REDEMPTION.
Look for it wherever
Harlequin Intrigue books are sold!

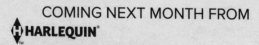

The door at the end of the train car opened and a man stepped through. Becca's pulse leaped. She reached out and gripped Quentin's leg. "Speak of the devil. He's headed this way. We need to hide. Right now." She shrank against Quentin's side, trying to get out of sight of the man heading directly toward them.

"Kiss me," Quentin urged.

"What?" She shot a glance at him. She'd wanted to kiss him all day long and wondered if he'd ever try to kiss her again. "Now?"

"Yes, now. Hurry." He swept the cap off her head, ruffled her hair, finger-combing it to let it fall around her shoulders in long, wavy curls. Then he gripped her arms and pulled her against him, pressing his lips to hers. Using her hair as a curtain to hide both of their faces, Quentin prolonged the kiss until Ivan passed them and walked through to the next car.

When the threat was gone, Quentin still did not let go of Becca. Instead, he pulled her across his lap and deepened the kiss.

Becca wrapped her arms around his neck. If Ivan came back that way, she never knew. All she knew was that if she died that moment, she'd die a happy woman. Quentin's kiss was that good.

The train lurched, throwing them out of the hold they had on each other. Becca lifted her head and stared around the interior of the train car. For the length of that soul-defining kiss, she'd forgotten about Ivan and the threat of starting a gunfight on a train full of people. Heat surged through her and settled low in her belly, and a profound ache radiated inside her chest. She wanted to kiss Quentin and keep kissing him. More than that, she wanted to make love to him and wake up beside him every day.

But she realized how impossible that would be. They were two very different people who worked in highly dangerous jobs, based out of different parts of the country. Nothing about a relationship with Quentin would work. She had to remind herself that he was a ladies' man—a navy guy with a female conquest in every port.

Don't miss A NAVY SEAL TO DIE FOR,
available October 2016 wherever
Harlequin® Intrigue books and ebooks are sold.

www.Harlequin.com